D0965690

Margaritas & Murder

A *Murder, She Wrote* Mystery

Margaritas & Murder

A *Murder, She Wrote* Mystery

A NOVEL BY

JESSICA FLETCHER & DONALD BAIN

Based on the Universal television series created by
Peter S. Fischer, Richard Levinson & William Link

 NEW AMERICAN LIBRARY

NEW AMERICAN LIBRARY
Published by New American Library, a division of
Penguin Group (USA) Inc., 375 Hudson Street,
New York, New York 10014, USA
Penguin Group (Canada), 90 Eglinton Avenue East, Suite 700, Toronto,
Ontario M4P 2Y3, Canada (a division of Pearson Penguin Canada Inc.)
Penguin Books Ltd., 80 Strand, London WC2R 0RL, England
Penguin Ireland, 25 St. Stephen's Green, Dublin 2,
Ireland (a division of Penguin Books Ltd.)
Penguin Group (Australia), 250 Camberwell Road, Camberwell, Victoria 3124,
Australia (a division of Pearson Australia Group Pty. Ltd.)
Penguin Books India Pvt. Ltd., 11 Community Centre, Panchsheel Park,
New Delhi - 110 017, India
Penguin Group (NZ), cnr Airborne and Rosedale Roads, Albany,
Auckland 1310, New Zealand (a division of Pearson New Zealand Ltd.)
Penguin Books (South Africa) (Pty.) Ltd., 24 Sturdee Avenue,
Rosebank, Johannesburg 2196, South Africa

Penguin Books Ltd, Registered Offices:
80 Strand, London WC2R 0RL, England

First published by New American Library,
a division of Penguin Group (USA) Inc.

First Printing, October 2005
1 3 5 7 9 10 8 6 4 2

Copyright © 2005 Universal Studios Licensing LLLP. Murder, She Wrote is a trademark
and copyright of Universal Studios.
All rights reserved

NEW AMERICAN LIBRARY and logo are trademarks of Penguin Group (USA) Inc.

LIBRARY OF CONGRESS CATALOGING-IN-PUBLICATION DATA:

Bain Donald, 1935–
Margaritas & murder : a Murder she wrote mystery : a novel / by Jessica Fletcher and Donald Bain.
p. cm.
ISBN: 0-451-21662-8
1. Fletcher, Jessica (Fictitious character)—Fiction. 2. Publishers and publishing—Crimes against
—Fiction. 3. Americans—Mexico—Fiction. 4. Women novelists—Fiction. 5. Kidnapping—
Fiction. 6. Mexico—Fiction. I. Title: Margaritas and murder. II Murder, she wrote (Television
Program) III. Title
PS3552.A376M25 2005
813'.54—dc22   2005013930

Set in Minion
Printed in the United States of America

Without limiting the rights under copyright reserved above, no part of this publication may be
reproduced, stored in or introduced into a retrieval system, or transmitted, in any form, or by any
means (electronic, mechanical, photocopying, recording, or otherwise), without the prior written
permission of both the copyright owner and the above publisher of this book.

PUBLISHER'S NOTE
This is a work of fiction. Names, characters, places, and incidents either are the product of the
author's imagination or are used fictitiously, and any resemblance to actual persons, living or dead,
business establishments, events, or locales is entirely coincidental.
  The publisher does not have any control over and does not assume any responsibility for author
or third-party Web sites or their content.

The scanning, uploading, and distribution of this book via the Internet or via any other means
without the permission of the publisher is illegal and punishable by law. Please purchase only
authorized electronic editions, and do not participate in or encourage electronic piracy of copy-
righted materials. Your support of the author's rights is appreciated

For Ted Chichak, with thanks

Margaritas
&
Murder

A *Murder, She Wrote* Mystery

Chapter One

"I don't have a formula as such for coming up with the plots for my novels. The ideas come from a variety of sources, really—a snatch of music that triggers a memory, a place I've visited, the news. If I find an article in the morning newspaper intriguing, I may clip it and file it away for future reference. Sometimes a person on a plane or train has an interesting face. I'll begin to imagine where that person is going, why she's frowning, and who will be waiting to pick her up at the station. Many of us do that, I suppose. It's human nature to be curious about those around us. I wish I had a more specific, useful answer to your question, but I'm afraid I don't."

The question had come from a woman in the front row, one of approximately a hundred people in the handsome room of a private library on Manhattan's West Side. I was on a panel of mystery writers—"crime writers" to the British—sponsored by the Authors Guild, of which I've been a proud and active member for many years. The guild is the closest thing writers have to a union, and it has initiated many legal actions against publishers when its leaders have felt writers have been treated unfairly. But the guild is more than that, sponsoring countless professional development seminars and panel discussions like the one I was on, and even managing a fund that can be tapped by members who find themselves in dire financial straits. It's a wonderful organization, and I always tried to make myself available when called upon.

Our moderator ended the session, and my fellow panelists and I spent another twenty minutes chatting with audience members who approached the dais. Finally, I was free to join my companions for the evening, Vaughan and Olga Buckley. Vaughan Buckley had been publishing my novels for many years. Our relationship had progressed from simply being publisher and author to being good friends as well. His wife had been a top fashion model when she met the dashing young editor who would go on to found Buckley House, a prestigious company and one of the last independent publishers that hadn't been gobbled up by an international conglomerate.

"Nicely done," Vaughan said as the three of us stepped out onto the hot pavement outside the library. New York was experiencing an early-summer heat wave. "Hungry?" he asked.

"As a matter of fact, I am," I said. "The interviews this afternoon backed up, and I never had lunch."

"The ecstasy of promoting a book," Olga said.

"And the agony," Vaughan said, chuckling. "Tell you what. Since we'll be in Mexico in another few days, I suggest we begin training our palate with some Mexican food, Manhattan style. They say the best way to combat the heat is to eat hot food. There's a good restaurant a block from here. Game?"

"Sure," I said.

We settled in a booth and Vaughan ordered margaritas, no salt.

"I must admit," I said, "Mexican food has never been my favorite."

"We don't have to stay," Olga said.

"Oh, no. There are always plenty of things on the menu that I like." I laughed. "You can take the girl out of Maine, but . . ."

"Maybe they serve lobster burritos," Vaughan offered.

"If they do," I said, "that's what I'll have. So tell me all about this Mexican hacienda you've ended up buying."

Vaughan and Olga looked at each other. Olga responded, "We fell madly in love with the highlands of central Mexico when we visited two years ago. We went back again, and last year we made a third visit. We were hooked. We decided—"

Vaughan interrupted. "It's not as much of a joint decision as Olga paints it."

"You love it there," she said, pretending to rap her husband's shoulder.

"Oh, yes, I do love it there. It's just that when you own a second home—we now have two—and it's in a lovely place like San Miguel de Allende, you want to spend as much time as possible there. It's a retirement paradise. But as appealing as that is, I'm just not ready to close up my office and spend all my days with my feet up on a lounge in the shade."

"I'm pleased to hear that," I said.

He placed his hand on my arm. "Not to worry, Jessica. As long as you keep writing novels, I'll keep publishing them."

Olga picked up where she'd left off. "It's more than four hundred fifty years old. The Mexican government has declared it a national monument—no traffic lights, neon signs, fire hydrants, or fast-food restaurants."

"All to the good—unless your house catches fire," Vaughan said.

"Or you have a sudden insatiable urge for a Big Mac," I added.

"It's become one of Mexico's leading centers for the arts," Olga said, ignoring our teasing. "The Instituto Allende Art School is world famous. The town is overflowing with artists, musicians, dancers, and actors. It's heaven." She pressed her hand to her heart to visually reinforce her ecstasy.

"It sounds wonderful," I said as the waiter placed menus in front of us.

"Do you have lobster?" Vaughan asked him.

"No, Señor," he said.

"Sorry," Vaughan said to me.

"Think nothing of it," I said. "Now, tell me about this house you've bought there."

"Let's order first," Olga said.

Our orders placed—I opted for ceviche, chicken fajitas, and a salad with tomatillo dressing—Vaughan said, "The house is very nice, Jessica, but you'll be seeing it in a few days. It was an incredible bargain. Living is cheap there. That's why there's a sizable expatriate community—'expats,' they call each other—Americans and Canadians looking to stretch their budgets and pensions. At last count there were almost five thousand of them living in the town and surrounding areas."

"We've already become friends with quite a few," Olga added. "They're a lively group, fond of saying that when you retire, you go to Florida to die, or to San Miguel to live. They all seem to be taking classes, getting together for parties, living their lives to the fullest."

"Well," I said as our first course was served, "you've certainly whetted my appetite for San Miguel de Allende. I'm even looking forward to this Mexican meal."

"Good," Vaughan said. "Let's have wine with dinner to celebrate our having enticed you, Jess, to spend a few weeks with us in Mexico. Maybe you'll fall in love with the place and buy the house next door."

"Maybe I will," I said, tasting the ceviche, a cold chopped seafood cocktail with onions, tomatoes, garlic, avocado, three kinds of peppers, and scallops "cooked" in lemon and lime juice. "Delicious!" I announced. "*Bueno!*"

Chapter Two

The Buckleys left for San Miguel de Allende before I did. Last-minute additions to my book-signing tour and an interview on the *Today* show, which was delayed two days due to a deluge of news coverage following the kidnapping and rescue of a world leader attending a conference in Cozumel, wreaked havoc with my travel schedule.

There were compensations. I had an extra day to shop for a special gift for my hosts. The Buckleys were voracious readers, of course, and I'd seen a lovely pair of bookends in Takashimaya on Fifth Avenue that I thought would appeal to them. In addition, the producer who'd arranged my appearance on *Today* tried to compensate for the inconvenience. Grateful for my "flexibility" regarding the change in plans, she gave me a few extra minutes with Katie Couric— more than originally planned—to talk about my new mystery and the life of a mystery writer. On my way out, she stopped me.

"We don't ordinarily do this," the producer said, handing me a videotape with a picture on the box of all the stars of the show, "but we really appreciate your willingness to stick around New York, especially considering the miserable weather we've been having. I apologize for the heat and humidity, even though there's nothing we can do about it."

"It was no bother at all to stay in town. Besides, I'm leaving tomorrow for sunny Mexico. I have a feeling the weather's not going to be much different there. A little drier, perhaps. Thank you for the tape. What's on it?"

"I thought you might like a souvenir of your interview with Katie."

"How thoughtful," I said. "I'll take it with me on the trip. I don't know if my friends get American television in Mexico, and I know they'd enjoy seeing this." I didn't mention that one of those friends was my publisher, who would have more than a passing interest in any publicity that might increase book sales, especially mine.

I was lucky to get a seat on a midmorning, four-hour flight to Mexico City. School was out and the tourist season had begun, filling planes to all the popular places. Olga and Vaughan had told me they usually took a bus from the Mexican capital to San Miguel, although they complained about its erratic timetable and the frequent breakdowns in the air-conditioning system.

"Fly to León instead," Olga had suggested. "You'll save hours of wear and tear on the road, and we'll send someone to pick you up." So I'd booked a connecting flight, and e-mailed the Buckleys my itinerary.

Upon landing in Mexico City, I learned the flight to León would be delayed. "Technical problems," a sympathetic gate agent said, shaking her head sadly. The plane wasn't leaving until that night. Since the bus was no longer an option—my luggage had been checked through to León, and there was no way to retrieve it—I resigned myself to the wait.

"Take a taxi to the zocalo," Vaughan said, when I called to relay the news of yet another delay in my travel plans. "It's a short cab ride, unless there's traffic. Maybe twenty or thirty minutes. But make sure you use the official cab stands. Don't take a ride from anyone who approaches you in the terminal. There have been a lot of tourist robberies in those kinds of taxis."

"Thank you," I said. "That's good to know."

"There's a beautiful café on the terrace of the Hotel Majestic. They have wonderful food and a spectacular view. Have a late lunch, relax, stroll around the square."

"Sounds wonderful."

"But if you do that, watch out for pickpockets. If you're wearing any jewelry, take it off and hide it somewhere on your person. And stay away from crowds. Perhaps you shouldn't purchase anything. You don't want to be flashing American money."

"I bought pesos before I left," I said, a little taken aback by all his warnings. "Maybe I should visit the Zona Rosa instead."

"I wouldn't. It's not the elegant neighborhood it once was. It fell into decay about twenty years ago. It's being gentrified all over again, but it's still a shadow of its former self and far too trendy for my liking," he said. "I hear Olga calling me. Listen, Jessica, just hang on to your pocketbook and have a good time. We'll see you later."

I hung up and wondered if I would be better off simply reading my book in the airport, but quickly discarded that idea. It had been many years since I'd visited Mexico City, but I remembered the beautiful architecture, the broad avenues, the wonderful museums, the exotic ruins, and the charming people. It was certainly worth giving the city the benefit of the doubt, I thought, as I joined the lines going through immigration.

The main hall of Benito Juárez International Airport in Mexico City is an immaculate monument to marble, with sweepers pushing long dry mops across the gleaming floors, every twenty feet it seemed, never allowing so much as a dust mote to land on the colorful stone. It was also jammed with people. The hub not only for flights to anywhere in Mexico but also for those to a good portion of Latin America, the airport handles more than twenty million passengers annually. It looked to me as if a million of them were there when I exited customs. They were leaning on the ropes that separated the travelers from those who welcomed them; crowding the souvenir shops, clothing stores, coffee bars, and magazine stands; jostling me as I walked the length of the terminal; and lining up outside at the "official" taxi stand, which was manned by yellow-jacketed staff who held clipboards. I stood in line to buy a ticket and waited in line again until it was my turn to climb into the back of the taxi, a small green car in which the front passenger seat had been removed, presumably to accommodate luggage, which I did not have. I told the driver the name of the hotel on the zocalo that Vaughan had recommended and leaned back against the cracked leather seat for the ride into town.

"Welcome to Mexico, Señora," the driver said. He pronounced it "meh-hee-co."

"Muchas gracias," I said, showing off the little Spanish I knew.

"Do you come for business or pleasure?"

"Definitely pleasure," I replied, smiling.

"You are traveling alone, yes?" He didn't wait for me to answer. "You must be very careful traveling alone in the city. There are some not nice people—*bandidos*—who will try to take advantage of you."

"So I've been told."

He leaned back in his seat, drew a card from his pocket, and handed it to me over his shoulder without taking his eyes from the road. "If you want someone reliable to take you around, show you all the beautiful and historic places, very cheap, you call me. I am Manuel Dias. I don't let anyone cheat you. I take good care of you. Guaranteed."

"That's very kind of you," I said, "but I'm not staying in Mexico City. In fact, I'm leaving this evening."

He clicked his tongue. "We are sorry to lose you," he said. "Where do you go? Acapulco? Cancún? I have a cousin in Mérida. Very good man."

"I'm going to San Miguel de Allende to visit friends.

They're sending someone to pick me up in León. My flight leaves this evening—at least I hope it will." It hadn't occurred to me till just then that I might have to stay overnight in Mexico City if the "technical problems" were not resolved. I wondered if I should buy an extra toothbrush just in case.

"This is terrible," the driver said.

"What's terrible?"

"I have no one for you in San Miguel. In León, maybe yes, I could find someone to help you. But you don't stay there."

"I appreciate your concern, but I'm sure I'll be just fine. My friends will take good care of me."

"You be careful going to San Miguel," he said, shaking a finger. "The country is no safer than the city."

"I'll remember that," I said, leaning forward and extending my arm. "Since I won't be needing it, here's your card."

"No, Señora. You keep it. You must go back to the airport tonight, yes? I will drive you. That way you'll be safe. Some taxis are not reliable. What time is your flight?"

I told him.

"Give my card to the desk at the hotel. They will call. I will pick you up right away. In Mexico we are very modern. I have the latest in technology." He held up a cell phone.

"That's a wonderful idea," I said. "I'll do that."

"But to be sure, you tell me what time to be at the hotel, and I will be waiting for you."

With Manuel Dias providing running commentary on

the places we passed along our way, we set out for the zocalo. The roads into the city funneled traffic from the wide boulevards of the outskirts, where he kept a heavy foot on the accelerator, to the clogged narrow streets around the downtown square. He guided us forward in agonizing inches, squeezing through impossible openings and cutting off myriad vehicles to move ahead. Other drivers shouted at him, furious, and he responded with equal vehemence. I was grateful I didn't understand what was being said and was convinced that the only reason the angry exchanges of the frustrated drivers didn't result in violence was that no one had enough room to open a door. The trip took over an hour, and I soon began calculating how much time I could realistically afford to spend in Mexico City before braving the traffic back to the airport to catch my flight. Manuel let me off on a side street around the corner from the front entrance of the hotel, instructing me to meet him at the same place when I was ready to leave. I had a feeling he wasn't going to move from that spot till I got back.

Vaughan's recommendation was a good one. The rooftop restaurant on the terrace of the Hotel Majestic not only overlooked the bustling zocalo—reputed to be one of the largest public plazas in the world, second only to Moscow's Red Square—but afforded a spectacular vista of the city beyond. The hostess ushered me to an empty table by a stone wall from which, by leaning forward, I could observe the goings-on in the plaza below or, by sitting back, rest my gaze on the city beyond it. The hot sun poured down on the terrace, but white umbrellas shaded the tables and a steady breeze made the air comfortable.

I ordered *pollo almendrado*—almond chicken—and a glass of orange juice. While I waited to be served, I peered over the wall and watched a group of youngsters dressed in traditional costumes doing an elaborate dance for a throng that encircled them in the square. The boys wore white pants and shirts with multicolored bands at their waists; the girls were in white dresses with black aprons and wore small headpieces with red ribbons that fluttered as they twirled around. Even from my perch seven floors above them, I could hear snatches of the music and the steady beat of a drum. A burst of applause greeted the end of their performance. They bowed to the audience, then ran to surround the man who had kept time with the drum, presumably their instructor, before he lined them up two by two and led them out of the square.

I opened my shoulder bag, pulled out a guidebook I'd bought in New York, and identified other buildings that bordered the zocalo. To my left was the Metropolitan Cathedral, a jumble of architectural styles that nevertheless resulted in an impressive baroque building with a pair of towers flanking one of several grand entrances. My book said it was begun in the sixteenth century to replace a cathedral built by Cortés and that it incorporates not only stones from the ruins of the Temple of Quetzalcoatl, an Aztec god, but also a wall of skulls of Aztec sacrificial victims. Taking up the entire east side of the plaza was the National Palace, built in the seventeenth century and home to government offices and Diego Rivera's celebrated murals depicting the history of Mexico. I glanced at my watch to see if there would be enough time to view the murals or stop at the cathedral. Maybe if I ate quickly, but it didn't look promising.

All thoughts of having a quick lunch evaporated a few minutes later when a mariachi band—two trumpets, two guitars, a violin, and a vocalist shaking maracas—stepped onto the terrace. I watched those around me look up happily as the band played the first notes of a song, the spirited music coaxing smiles from even the most serious diners. The waiter brought a basket of bread and kept my glass filled with juice until my chicken was served. I ate and listened to the band members as they threaded their way between the umbrellas to serenade each of the tables, my foot keeping time with the lively beat.

The music helped ease the tension of my hectic last few weeks. It was nice to be on vacation. I love to travel, but book tours can be exhausting—a real "if this is Tuesday, it must be Boston" experience. While I enjoy meeting new people, especially readers, seeing new places, and learning about them, it's always a pleasant prospect to contemplate a few weeks with nothing specific to do but sit back and relax. No notes to take, no schedules to meet, no rush to catch another plane. Vaughan and Olga were the perfect hosts. They had a busy life of their own, and they insisted I was to use their home as if it were mine and join them—or not—as I wished. They had promised that I wouldn't be in their way. "We'll even ignore you if that's what you want."

Which, of course, wasn't what I wanted at all. What I did want was time. Time to renew our acquaintance. Time to stretch out with a book. Time to take leisurely walks in a charming town. Perhaps some gallery or museum visits, or a concert I could treat them to. Just a peaceful vacation with old friends. It sounded wonderful. But I was in for a rude awakening.

Chapter Three

"The airport is closing?"

"Sí, Señora. We close so we can clean the terminal."

"But my ride to San Miguel de Allende isn't here yet."

The terminal agent shrugged. My problems were not his problems.

The flight to León had taken off an hour late. I arrived at Del Bajio Airport at eleven p.m. and thankfully found my luggage a half hour later. One by one, other passengers on the flight had picked up their bags and disappeared into the night. I'd searched in vain for someone holding a cardboard placard with my name on it and had waited patiently at first, convinced that whoever was picking me up was merely running late. After an hour, pacing in front of the airport's glass doors, I had my doubts. I hesitated to telephone the Buckleys. When I'd called from Mexico City to tell of them about the second delay, Olga had assured me it was no problem. Carlos would be there to pick me up. He was a little flaky, she admitted, but he'd always come through for them. They would be out earlier in the evening at a party but were planning to be home to greet me. In fact they would leave the front door unlocked, just in case they got delayed. My guest room, straight ahead at the top of the stairs, was already made up. They'd see me in the morning.

Reluctantly, I dialed them again to tell them of my predicament, but they weren't home. I left a message on the answering machine.

"There is a bench outside, Señora. You are welcome to sit there till your driver comes," the agent said.

I had visions of sleeping—or not sleeping—on a bench outside the airport terminal. And how would I recognize Carlos if he eventually showed up? I didn't even know his last name, much less what kind of car he drove.

"Can you call a taxi to take me to San Miguel de Allende?" I asked.

"They're all gone."

"Gone?"

"Sí, Señora. The passengers from your flight, they take them all. There are no more taxicabs here. They know we clean the terminal now."

"Is there a hotel within walking distance?"

"All the hotels in the city are full." He shrugged again. "It is the tourist season."

A man who'd been mopping the floor called across the terminal to the agent, who cocked his head to one side. A brief debate ensued, but I had no idea what they spoke about. "Hokay," the agent finally said, turning to me. "Pablo's son will drive you."

My faith in the goodness of people soared. It has often been my experience that when someone needs help, someone else will step forward to offer it. In my travels, I've learned that people are the same the world over, some good, some not. But most are generous, friendly, and willing to provide assistance, even if they haven't been asked. It certainly was true of my hometown of Cabot Cove. People in Maine can be standoffish to those they don't know. But if someone needs help—even a stranger—they will be the first to extend a hand. I gave the man with the mop a grateful smile. *"Gracias,"* I said.

"De nada," he said, leaning his mop against the wall and drawing a cell phone from a holster hooked to his belt. He spoke into the phone, frowned, and raised his voice. Holding the phone between his shoulder and his ear, he looked up at me and raised both hands, showing ten fingers. *"Diez minutos."*

Ten minutes. I heaved a sigh of relief.

"You can wait on that bench," the agent said. "I will tell you when Juanito, he is here."

I thanked the agent, rolled my suitcase over to the wooden bench near the terminal entrance, sat down, and rummaged in my shoulder bag for the notebook in which I'd written Olga and Vaughan's San Miguel street address and telephone number. I tore a blank sheet from the book, wrote the Buckleys' address on it, and tucked the book back in my bag.

Juanito arrived fifteen minutes later. He couldn't have been more than seventeen. A lanky boy with jet-black hair sticking up in spikes on the top of his head, he wore blue jeans, sandals, and a green Tommy Hilfiger T-shirt. He looked as if he'd just gotten out of bed, and given the yawn he tried to stifle, I suspected that might actually have been the case. I felt two things: sorry that his father had had to awaken him to accommodate me and grateful that I would not have to spend the night in the airport.

Juanito jingled his car keys in front of my face. "San Miguel de Allende? Sí?"

"Sí," I said.

He grabbed my bag and rolled it out the door before I had a chance to get to my feet. I followed him outside to a dusty white convertible with large black patches on the fenders and a tear in the top. The trunk made a squealing noise when he opened it. He flung my bag inside and slammed the lid shut with both hands, bouncing on it to add his weight and make certain it stayed closed. He held open the door to the rear seat, and I slid in. There was no seat belt, but given the vintage of the car, I would have been foolish to expect one.

When he climbed into the driver's seat, I asked, *"¿Habla inglés?"* hoping he spoke English.

"No, Señora. *¿Habla español?*"

"Not really," I muttered, shaking my head. My Spanish was more than rusty. It had gaping holes in it, like Juanito's car. I leaned forward and handed him the paper on which I'd written Vaughan and Olga's address.

He nodded, folded the sheet twice, stuck it under a rubber band holding the fabric of the sun visor in place, started the engine, and we roared out of the airport. But we didn't go far. Juanito pulled into the first gas station we came to, a squat building illuminated by a bare lightbulb over the door, with two ancient gas pumps in front. Several men sat on barrels outside the door, smoking and drinking beer. Juanito went into the office, returned with two cans of oil, and poured them into the thirsty engine.

The men ignored Juanito and his vehicle until something interesting caught the attention of one. He lurched to his feet and stumbled in the direction of the car, calling over his shoulder to his companions, who laughed. At the door to the backseat, he hunched down to get a better look at Juanito's passenger, the fumes from his alcoholic breath filling the car. My hand crept into my shoulder bag and my fingers encircled a can of hair spray I'd picked up in the Mexico City airport while waiting for the flight to León. It wasn't Mace, but it would do in a pinch.

"*Buenas noches,*" I said with a tight smile.

The man growled something I knew I wouldn't want translated and leered at me.

Juanito yelled at him, pulled two crumpled bills from his pocket, and stuffed them in the man's hands, nearly knocking him over in his efforts to push him away from the car.

Fortified, we left León and headed toward San Miguel. At first I was grateful to be on the road and I tried to ignore the speed at which Juanito drove. It occurred to me he may have been trying to reach our destination before the car ran out of oil again. But I was wrong. He stopped again a half hour into our trip to replenish the oil supply. After that, we were on our own. There were no more service stations. There were no more paved roads. We were in the mountains.

I wondered if Juanito had taken a shortcut or if this was actually the highway to San Miguel de Allende. It certainly didn't look as if it accommodated a lot of traffic. The road was a narrow and winding roller coaster carved into the sides of low hills, with rocks and brush for borders, rarely steep for very long but with enough twists and turns to challenge the bravest fun seeker. Later the land flattened out, allowing Juanito to press harder on the accelerator. The countryside flew by, our headlights reflecting off the flanks of many a cow grazing nearby or occasionally wandering onto the road itself.

It seemed to me that the farther away from León we got, the faster Juanito drove. We passed through tiny towns, hurtling down the main thoroughfare of each one. Speeding up rather than slowing down when locals appeared by the side of the road, we raced along the dry trails, leaving a plume of dust in our wake.

I clung to the top of the front seat and braced my hand on the door, struggling to stay upright in the rocketing car. Desperate, I tried to remember the Spanish words meaning "please slow down"; I settled on yelling *"Por favor, no mas rapido"* over the roar of the engine and praying that Juanito would understand. He answered me in rapid-fire Spanish, the only word of which I grasped was *"bandidos."*

Bandits! He was worried about bandits.

He looked around to reassure me, grinned, and held up what to him must have been a trusty weapon. It was a baseball bat. Good heavens! I could see the headline: AMERICAN TOURIST AND MEXICAN BOY FACE OFF AGAINST BANDITS WITH A CAN OF HAIR SPRAY AND A LOUISVILLE SLUGGER. After that, I held on and squeezed my eyes shut, opening them only to peer at my watch every few minutes, a wasted exercise because it was too dark to see the dial.

"San Miguel," Juanito sang out some time later.

I looked up. The car had crested a hill, and there, nestled in the valley below, were the sparkling lights of a good-sized city.

"Wonderful," I said, relieved that this harrowing ride would soon be over. The town looked as if it wasn't too far off, and I estimated we could be at the Buckleys' in fifteen minutes or so. I wondered what their house would look like. We had never discussed that. Would it be a Spanish-style stucco with dark beams jutting from the eaves? Or would it be built of brick or stone with long, narrow windows, or perhaps with filigreed iron balconies? I pictured Olga in a long caftan, floating through a room with high ceilings and whitewashed walls dominated by oil paintings. She was an elegant woman, tall and slender with a deportment that suggested royalty, a perception that Vaughan delighted in, knowing the real woman. Many people were intimidated by her at first, but that didn't last long if they took the time to look beyond first impressions. She was warm and sweet, and made an effort to see to the comfort of everyone around her. Of course, I also knew her silly side. She was a great mimic and had a devilish laugh that was infectious. Her house would be—well, I couldn't think what it would be. I knew one thing: It would be a welcome sight regardless of its architecture and décor.

The fifteen minutes came and went. The lights of San Miguel in front of us became lights to the side of us, and eventually lights behind, as Juanito maneuvered the car down the tortuous mountain road. By that time I was too tired to be fearful of his driving anymore. Instead, I day-dreamed—or should it be nightdreamed—imagining my-self already at our destination. I saw myself tiptoeing up the stairs to Vaughan and Olga's guest room, trying not to awaken them, sinking into the freshly made bed and sleep-ing deeply. Just the thought of cool sheets and a soft pillow relaxed me. The ride had been an adventure I could recount in the morning over coffee. Vaughan loved a good story, and I thought of ways I could embellish it for his amuse-ment. Not that it required much embellishment. But my vi-sion was instantly shattered when we rounded a curve to find a boulder in the center of the road.

Juanito swerved to the right, the wheels of the car climbing the rocks bordering the shoulder. I slid across the bench seat and slammed into the door. Thank goodness it didn't open. We careened ahead, balancing on two wheels, the low-hanging branches of trees reaching through the open window, grabbing at our clothes and scraping the top and sides of the car, sounding like the screeching of chalk on a blackboard. Juanito cut the wheel sharply and the car righted itself, jouncing over the rough surface, and came to a stop before two trees, the headlights riding up and down their trunks in smaller and smaller waves as the car's movement settled. Suddenly, it seemed, the only sound I heard was the hiss of steam escaping the radiator. The engine had died.

Juanito, his face ashen, released a stream of Spanish curses and pounded the steering wheel with both hands.

"Juanito, are you all right?" I asked.

My hands were shaking. A hundred questions flashed through my mind. How would we get to San Miguel now? I couldn't see the lights of the city anymore. Did that mean we were closer to level ground? Perhaps we could walk the rest of the way. Were we near a home on the outskirts of the city? Could we call for help? I had a cell phone. Would it work in the mountains of central Mexico? Did Juanito have a cell phone, too? Did the police patrol the highways around San Miguel? Were we stuck here till someone found us? How long would that be?

I took inventory of my body. I felt no pain, but my heart was pounding. I knew I might possibly be in shock but doubted I had any serious injury. We hadn't struck anything, even though the car had taken positions more appropriate to stunt driving than to cross-country travel. I guessed I would be sore the next day, however. When I'd banged into the door, the window crank had given me a good poke in the hip.

"Juanito?" I said again. "Are you all right?"

He was silent. But he seemed to be straining to hear.

He doesn't speak English, Jessica, I reminded myself. *"Cómo está usted?"* I asked. How are you? Not exactly the correct question, but perhaps he would understand my meaning.

He didn't answer, but he whipped around, his eyes wide, as the back door flew open and I was yanked into the night.

Chapter Four

The man who pulled me from the car was, unfortunately, not a policeman. Medium height and stocky, he was dressed in dark clothing—I'd say black if I had to guess. It was a moonlit night, but even so, colors were hard to distinguish. I could see that he wore a plaid bandanna over his nose and mouth and a hat that was more cowboy than sombrero. The bandanna must have limited his access to air, or else he'd had to run to catch up with the car; he breathed heavily, wheezing as he flung me aside to open the driver's door and train the muzzle of a revolver on Juanito. Despite the thief's breathlessness, his intent was clear to the young man, who got out slowly, his hands raised in the air. I was relieved to see he'd left his baseball bat on the seat. It was no match for a gun.

Juanito looked at me apologetically. In response to the outlaw's command, he dug into the pockets of his jeans and pulled out a handful of coins. The man snarled at him, gave a slight cough, and aimed his gun at me.

I turned out the pockets of my suit jacket, but the only item in them was the card from Manuel Dias, my cabdriver in Mexico City, which I held up to show the bandit. He stepped forward to see what it was, knocked it out of my hand, and backed away, hoarsely barking an order.

"*Habla inglés?*" I said, doubting that he could speak English and, truthfully, hoping that he didn't. If he was limited in his ability to communicate with me, I could pretend ignorance of what he wanted. On the other hand, it also made it more difficult for me to gauge what he intended to do, although it was evident that robbery, at a minimum, was on his mind.

The bandit raised his voice but was seized with a coughing fit. Afraid his gun might go off accidentally, I tried to sidestep out of range.

He waved the weapon at me, indicating he wanted me to move closer to Juanito, cleared his throat, and tried again.

"*No hablo español,*" I said slowly, trying to give it my worst American accent. "I don't speak Spanish."

"*Dinero,*" he managed to grind out. "*Dólares, moneda, pesos.*"

I understood that he wanted money and I pointed to the car. "My purse is in there," I said.

He said something to Juanito, who took my elbow and pulled me farther away from the car. The bandit glanced inside and looked back quickly, keeping his weapon on us. He saw my shoulder bag but was leery of reaching for it himself; he directed Juanito to get it for him.

The man was clearly sick. He was having difficulty breathing, particularly since the bandanna restricted his oxygen. He shuddered as another cough wracked his body, and he lifted the triangular bottom of the cloth so he could inhale through his mouth, a mistake that sent him into another paroxysm of coughing. I watched him carefully but couldn't make out the shape of his chin. Still, as my eyes became accustomed to the available light, I tried to observe whatever I could that might help me identify him, should I have the opportunity. I could see that he was soft around the middle, as if he were dressed in multiple layers of clothing. The night was cool, but not so cool that it required a heavy jacket. Was it part of his disguise, an attempt to hide his physique? Or maybe he was homeless and wearing his entire wardrobe to keep it from being stolen. That's not unusual. In some of our largest cities, where homeless shelters are no haven from thieves, poor people can't take a chance on leaving any item of clothing where someone else might find it.

He must be desperate, I thought, to stake out a lonely road in the middle of the night on the remote chance that a car would come by and its occupants would have anything he considered worthwhile. I hadn't seen another car since we left León. How had he gotten here? Did he have a car or truck stashed somewhere out of sight? Or had he walked up from town to set his trap? The boulder Juanito had swerved to avoid had not gotten in our way by itself. No ledge of rocks loomed over the road—only brush and scrub trees and dry dirt.

Unless an accomplice waited in a getaway car nearby, the bandit appeared to be alone. Had there been more than one, and had I not been so weary after a day of traveling and suffering one delay after another—this one being intolerable—I might not have reacted so boldly.

Juanito backed out of the car, dragging my shoulder bag by the strap. The bandit instructed him to dump the contents on the road, and the boy obeyed.

"That's really not necessary," I said, as out tumbled my wallet, guidebook, notebook, two pens, flashlight, hair spray, tissue packet, a roll of Life Savers, house keys, a tube of sunscreen, the extra toothbrush I'd just purchased, pocket comb, glasses case, luggage lock, foldable sun hat, a packet of cookies from the morning flight, combination mirror/magnifier, and my favorite lipstick, which rolled under the car.

My wallet was easily visible, but the bandit ignored it. Instead, he poked his boot through my possessions, kicking aside my sun hat, crushing the cookies, and putting his foot down on the mirror.

"I hope you're not superstitious," I said tartly. "Some people think that's seven years' bad luck."

He squinted at me and stomped down till all that was left was splinters.

"Stop it!" I said. "This is not a game." I hadn't been a schoolteacher for nothing. The tone of my voice caught the thief by surprise. I leaned down and picked up my wallet, opened it, took out the remainder of the pesos I had gotten in New York before I left, and thrust the money at him. It was all I was carrying. I had traveler's checks in my luggage, but they would do him no good, and I wasn't about to volunteer the one credit card I carried.

"You wanted the money. Now take it."

He grabbed the bills from my hand and jumped back, as if I were about to attack.

"It isn't necessary to destroy other people's property," I said. "You should be ashamed, holding up a woman who could be your mother and a boy less than half your age. Some macho man you are. You've gotten what you came for. Now leave us alone and go."

I took my bag from Juanito, put the wallet inside, and glared at the thief. He may have had a limited understanding of English, but he was perceptive enough to recognize sarcasm when he heard it and the word *macho* was not lost on him. Not about to lose face in front of a boy, he growled something at Juanito, who pointed to the watch on my wrist.

I unhooked the clasp, regretting that I hadn't listened to Vaughan and hidden my jewelry where it wouldn't be seen.

He waved the gun at my earrings. I removed them and gave them and the watch to Juanito, who handed them to the bandit.

He grunted, looked over my person, noticed a ring I was wearing, and gestured toward it with his gun.

"Absolutely not!" I said.

"Señora," Juanito said, looking from me to the man worriedly.

"No," I said, shaking my head. The ring had been a gift

to me from my late husband, Frank. It was not particularly valuable, but it had great sentimental meaning. Perhaps I was being foolish. Certainly I was—after all, the man had a gun—but I was not about to part with it.

The *bandido* shouted and held up the gun, aiming at Juanito's head. That he might kill the boy if I didn't turn over the ring horrified me. Quickly I slipped it from my finger and held it out to him. "Take it. Take it," I said, fury in my voice. He grabbed the ring and took a step back, but was hampered by another fit of coughing. He waved the gun around in the air even while he was gasping for breath, but was unable to control the air coming into or leaving his lungs, his shoulders and back jerking with the spasms.

I took advantage of his momentary incapacity to kneel and gather my belongings. On my knees in the dust of the mountains of central Mexico, I picked up the scattered items, brushed them off, and tucked them back into my shoulder bag. The mirror was a complete loss, but I didn't want to leave the shards where they were, so I made a neat pile of the pieces and wrapped them in a tissue. Juanito knelt beside me. He apologized in a low voice and reached under the car to retrieve my lipstick.

I picked up the hair spray and shook the can. I hesitated only a moment. A man with a gun was dangerous. He hadn't squeezed the trigger yet, but there were no assurances that he wouldn't. What was he planning to do with us? Had my pique so angered him that I'd increased the odds of his harming us, perhaps even killing us? I couldn't take that chance. If anything happened to Juanito, I would be responsible. He had behaved appropriately. I had not. Any law enforcement expert will tell you that it's always prudent to cooperate with the person holding a weapon, to obey his orders and not to antagonize him further. I was the one who'd broken the rules, who'd challenged our captor. If we got out of this in one piece, I swore to myself, I would make more of an effort to stop plunging headlong into trouble.

It was too late for prudence now. I flipped off the cap with my thumb and rose, fully intending to aim a stream of lacquer at the robber's face. My hope was that the spray would take him by surprise, set off another round of coughing, or sting his eyes enough that Juanito and I could wrest the gun from his fingers.

In one smooth movement I raised the can, depressed the button, and turned to where the *bandido* had been curled over, trying to catch his breath. The hiss of the spray was loud in the silent night. But it didn't find its mark. The man was gone. He had crept away while we were the most vulnerable, on our knees in the dirt. We heard the sounds of his retreat as he escaped down the mountain, crashing through the brush, boots skidding over rocks, his cough echoing back to us.

Chapter Five

"Oh, Jessica, I'm so sorry. I can't believe Carlos never showed up and we weren't home to take your call. He's never done that before. He's usually reliable."

Vaughan shot his wife a look that clearly questioned her statement.

"He *did* leave us a message saying that his car had broken down and that he couldn't find anyone willing to take his place," Olga said. "I can't believe the airport closed and there were no taxis. If only I'd known. We never should have gone to that party."

"There was nothing you could have done from so far away, Olga. Besides, Juanito's father solved the problem of transportation by sending him to pick me up. It would have worked out perfectly if we hadn't been waylaid."

We were in the Buckleys' elegant dining room, having a very late meal. There were dark beams overhead, the rich wood matched by the tall chairs surrounding the long farmhouse table. The walls had been washed with a soft ocher, and the color gathered in the crevices of the hand-plastered surface, emphasizing its intentionally uneven texture. As I had imagined, there were paintings hanging everywhere, but they were not the ponderous dark oils I had pictured. These were light, cheerful canvases of flowers and houses and scenes from what was probably the artist's life in San Miguel.

I leaned against the striped silk upholstery of the chair and rested my elbows on its arms. Olga and her housekeeper, Maria Elena, had set the table with a colorful serape on which they'd placed plates of food, bottles of wine, and tall iron candlesticks with fat red candles. While they were preparing their impromptu banquet, I took a much-desired bath to wash the dust out of my hair and the tension out of my shoulders. I was tired but at the same time extraordinarily alert. I needed sleep—it was close to four in the morning—but knew that it was unlikely to come, since my mind was racing, replaying the scenes with the bandit as if they were part of a movie I couldn't turn off.

"When we came home late and realized you still weren't here, I was so worried. I wanted Vaughan to call Carlos at his house, but of course what good would that have done? We assumed you'd hired a car, and were terrified that you might have gotten into an accident. But to think you'd been the victim of *bandidos*! I don't know which is worse."

"One *bandido*, and no real harm done, except maybe to Juanito's car." I took a sip of the tea that Maria Elena had kindly made for me.

"But he took your money."

"Actually, I gave it to him. If we had to testify in a court of law, he would have a good case claiming I donated the money."

"But your watch and your earrings and your ring."

"Now, there he'd be in trouble. Those I surrendered at the point of a gun," I said, thinking about the ring Frank had given me. "My husband gave me that ring when we were courting," I said, touching the finger where until recently I'd worn the gold band with three tiny rubies. "I would have fought hard to keep it, but I couldn't jeopardize Juanito's life."

"Of course not," Olga said. "We'll absolutely replace the other jewelry. I'll take you shopping first thing in the morning."

"Second thing will be time enough," Vaughan said, putting his hand on my arm and giving me a gentle squeeze. "We're just grateful you're all right and are finally here."

"I am, too," I said. "Can you believe my driver and I both had cellular phones but neither one of them worked? I guess we were too far out of range for service."

"To be robbed at gunpoint and abandoned on the road—" Olga shuddered at the thought. "I just can't take it in. We've heard the rumors, but we never knew anyone it actually happened to before." She turned to her husband. "Let that be a lesson to you, Vaughan."

"Not now, Olga."

"I don't know what we would have done if the police hadn't found you, Jessica."

"We were certainly happy to see those flashing lights," I said, smiling. "Thank you for calling them."

Juanito's efforts to restart his car had been futile. We'd both leaned under the hood, I aiming my flashlight at the engine while he jiggled wires, checked the oil, and opened and closed several caps, the uses for which I hadn't the faintest idea. He tried to coax the motor to life for the better part of an hour, even putting me in the driver's seat and gesturing to indicate when I should try turning the key or pressing on the accelerator. For two people who didn't speak the same language and one who had never driven a car—me—we communicated very well.

I had resigned myself to spending the rest of the night sleeping in the backseat when I saw the reflection of lights bouncing off trees as the patrol car made its way up the mountain. I shook Juanito's shoulder and he raced to the middle of the road, frantically waving his arms to flag them down.

The officers had delivered me to the Buckleys'—Juanito had led them there—and used the services of Maria Elena to translate instructions that I was to go to the *delegación*, the police station, the following afternoon to make a formal report to the chief of police. They gave me a card with his name and office address.

The Buckleys had offered to put Juanito up for the night, but he had declined, saying he had an uncle in town who would take him in and help him repair his car, according to Maria Elena's translation.

She was a small, compact woman with large brown eyes

in a round face. Her long gray hair was pulled into a braid that hung down her back against the robe she had thrown over her nightclothes. After the police had left, she had fussed over me, running the water for my bath, unpacking my suitcase, making me tea, and bringing out platters of meat and vegetable turnovers, fresh salads, and warm bread, which the Buckleys nibbled at as well.

"This is wonderful, Maria Elena," I said. "With all the delays, I never managed to eat dinner."

"I must apologize," she said. "I am very distressed at what happened to you in my country."

"Mexico has no monopoly on crime," I replied. "This could have occurred anywhere in the world. As luck would have it, most of what was lost can be replaced, and thankfully no one was injured."

"Even so, there is too much crime in my country. Father Alfredo says the government is not doing enough to protect our citizens, much less our visitors."

"I wasn't aware of problems here," Olga said. "I've heard of things being stolen when people are away, but no violent crime."

"In San Miguel it is safe, but outside, maybe not," Maria Elena said. "The police, they blame the poor people, but it is not the poor who kidnap or kill. These are professional criminals. They make money by holding tourists for ransom, but sometimes they don't keep their part of the bargain. It is very bad."

"Well, thank goodness that wasn't the case tonight," Vaughan said. "I think this discussion is better left for the morning, Jessica. You must be exhausted, and we can all use some sleep."

"I can't argue with that," I said, rising. "Let me help you clear away the dishes."

"No, no, Señora. That is my job."

"I'll help Maria Elena," Olga said. "Vaughan, why don't you show Jessica to her room?" She gave me a peck on the cheek and pushed me toward the hall. "I'll see you in the morning. Better yet, sleep late and I'll see you in the afternoon."

"May I get you anything else, Señora?" Maria Elena asked me.

"No, thank you. I think I have everything I need."

I took Vaughan's arm and he escorted me up a flight of stairs, pausing outside the door to the guest room.

"She's a lovely woman," I said.

"Maria Elena?"

"Yes. She was a wonderful help translating what the police were saying."

"Lucky for all of us. My Spanish is limited, although Olga and I are taking a class at the Instituto Allende."

"She's a terrific cook, too. I hadn't realized how hungry I was until she brought in—what were they exactly? They were wonderful."

"Those were empanadas, Jessica. My favorite. I can eat them by the dozen."

"I think they'll become my favorite, too."

"I'll bet they tasted even better now that you know you'll be around to eat them again." He raised an eyebrow at me. "Kidding aside, Jessica, are you all right? That was a traumatic experience you had this evening."

"I'm fine, Vaughan."

"I know you've been in a lot of scrapes over the years, but this . . ."

"I promise you, I'm perfectly well. Now, tell me, how did you meet Maria Elena? From what I understood, you're only here a short time, and you don't stay for very long when you are."

"Her brother Hector helped us with the renovations. He said his sister was a recent widow and was looking for work. We were lucky when she agreed to live here full-time. We told her to make the house her own when we're away, entertain if she wants, just enjoy the amenities. I have a wonderful media room, complete with satellite TV, computer hookup, and a multimedia surround-sound system."

"You do?"

Vaughan laughed. "I'm an electronics buff. It's a passion of mine." I must have looked surprised because he added, "Never knew that about me, did you?"

"I had no idea."

"I can't be an effete snob all the time, Jessica. I have to do something manly every now and then. I installed most of the equipment myself, with a little help from a fellow I met here, Eric Gewirtz. He's a computer expert, down with his family for the summer. Nice guy. Really knows his stuff. Would you like to see the room? It's just down the hall."

"Of course I would. This is a part of your personality

you've been keeping secret from me. What does Olga think of your passion?"

"She's been tolerating it for years, but while our apartment at the Dakota has thick walls, it isn't soundproofed." Vaughan ushered me inside a large room and closed a padded door behind us. "Welcome to my playroom. That's what Olga calls it. It's an apt name. I can tinker with my toys and play my music any time of the day or night without disturbing the neighbors, or my wife."

"It's impressive," I said, turning in a circle to take in Vaughan's installation. One wall was floor-to-ceiling wall-to-wall cabinetry in three parts. The center section was composed of several panels of beautiful wood doors. Flanking them were exposed shelves neatly filled with compact disks, DVDs, videotapes, and of course books. Two columns of shelves held stacks of black equipment behind dark glass.

Vaughan patted the closed doors. "I had them use cocobolo for the cabinets. It's Mexican lumber similar to rosewood. I've tried to use native materials wherever I could. Since we're taking advantage of the Mexican economy, I figured I should contribute to it as well."

"Very admirable," I said.

"Come sit. I'll show you how everything works."

Vaughan led me to a long sectional sofa facing the shelves. Made of soft gray suede, it ran the entire wall, ending on one side in a chaise longue. Two large ottomans pushed together doubled as a cocktail table and held a silver tray containing half a dozen remote control devices. The wall opposite the door was draped in black velvet.

The décor was decidedly masculine, but I could see Olga's touches in the colorful pillows that were piled up on the chaise and scattered along the back of the sofa, and in the wildly patterned rug that sat atop the gray carpet.

"Let's see. What can I show you first?" Vaughan said, picking up a remote. In response to the buttons he pressed, the double doors in the center of the cabinet slid silently to the sides to reveal a television with a huge screen.

"It's an HD cinema wall, plasma monitor," he said proudly, "with component video to minimize distortion and composite video carrying luminescence, chrominance, and raster synchronizing information."

"Are we still speaking English?" I asked, laughing.

"Wait till you see it," he said. "It also has Dolby digital AC3 surround sound." He pushed another button. A picture bloomed on the screen—a video of a man in a white sombrero and an ornamented Mexican jacket leading a magnificent dappled gray horse. Lively music poured from speakers positioned in every corner of the room.

"Isn't it great?" Vaughan shouted over the music. "That's an Ezequiel Peña DVD. He's a mariachi and *ranchera* singer. Can you hear the violins coming out of that speaker and the trumpets from this one?"

"It's wonderful," I said. "Can you turn it down a bit?"

Vaughan smiled sheepishly and lowered the volume. "I like it loud," he said, "but I understand that not everyone does."

"It's a remarkably sharp picture," I said.

"It can serve as my computer monitor, too," he said,

switching off the DVD to a blank screen. "I've got a cordless keyboard on that shelf over there that's a gem. I just put up my feet and surf the Internet."

"All the comforts of home," I said, reaching for a different remote. "What else can these marvels of technology do?"

"Try it and see."

I pushed a button and the lights dimmed; I pushed another and the velvet hangings drew aside to reveal a bank of broad windows.

"You can't really tell now because it's still dark outside, but the drapes eliminate ninety percent of the ambient light," he said. "Makes a big difference in the picture."

I pressed the button to close them again, raised the lighting, and put the device back with its brothers.

"Those are infrared—pretty common," Vaughan said, reaching for a silver case, "but this one operates on radio frequency, so it works through doors and walls. I can control the music in every room in the house from right here."

"I have one remote at home, and I'm not sure what all the buttons do," I said. "How do you keep track of it all?"

"Easy. Look here. I put instructions on the back."

He handed me the remote. I held out my arm and squinted at the tiny type, but it remained illegible.

"I can't read this without my glasses," I said.

"Here, try mine," Vaughan said, handing me his reading glasses. "It's really not as hard as you think once you know which remote controls which equipment, and I've labeled each one."

"I'll have to take your word for it," I said.

"You sound like Olga. But it's fun once you get the hang of it. Maria Elena knows how to operate all this stuff. I gave her lessons, hoping she would use it for her own entertainment."

"And does she?"

"I doubt it. I'm afraid she only lives in her own rooms and the kitchen when we're not here. I wish she'd take advantage of the rest of the house. It's silly just to keep it dusted for the two or three times a year we can get here."

"I think I can understand that, though. It's not hers."

"True. But I was hoping she wouldn't feel that way. We wouldn't want this house if she weren't here to help us out."

"It's beautiful. I'm looking forward to seeing the rest of it tomorrow."

"Speaking of tomorrow, it's almost here. I'm sorry. You must be beat, and I've kept you from your bed with my toys."

"I loved seeing them. You'll have to show me how to get my e-mail tomorrow."

"My pleasure."

Vaughan shut off the equipment and closed the door on the playroom. In the hallway I remembered something that had struck me earlier. I put a hand on his arm. "Do you mind if I ask you a question?"

"Not at all."

"What did Olga mean when we were talking about the *bandido* and she said, 'Let that be a lesson to you'?"

"Nothing at all to worry about. I'm going on the mail run. That's all."

"What's the mail run?"

"It's too long a story before bed. I'll tell you all about it tomorrow. For now, just get a good night's rest—what's left of it—and sleep late. You had a rough trip here, but the worst is over. The rest of your vacation is going to be nothing but relaxation and fun."

I bid him good night and was soon sound asleep in the guest room, Vaughan's words echoing in my brain. But the worst *wasn't* over, as I would soon find out.

It was yet to come.

Chapter Six

The San Miguel police station was on the north side of a lovely park in the center of town. Called El Jardin, or the garden, it was a neat square, with municipal buildings on one side and La Parroquia, an elegant Gothic-style pink stone church with slender spires, on the other. Carefully tended laurel trees provided shade over the park's pathways and green iron benches, every one of which was occupied by men and women, old and young, chatting, sipping coffee, reading newspapers, and watching the excitement on the faces of children as they jumped up and down at the approach of a balloon vendor. El Jardin was the city's geographic hub, but it was also its social center, and we stopped often so Olga could introduce me to people she knew and point out others whose acquaintance she'd made in the short time she and Vaughan had been homeowners.

"There's Jim Sullivan and Deb Gerrity. They run a gallery over on Correo, not too far from here. Deb's daughter, Emilie, is a prima ballerina with the American Ballet Theatre. That pretty lady with the dark hair, over there, is Lee Barette. She was a postmaster up north—she won't let me say 'postmistress.' Now she's teaching yoga to the retirees. I found her name on a bulletin board at one of the cafés. She lets me sit in, in a manner of speaking, whenever we're down here."

"How nice," I said.

"It is. Other than walking around town, her class is the only exercise I get."

I laughed. "I would say walking around town is nothing to sniff at. It was quite a hike from your home to here, but I think you took the long way around."

"True, but I wanted you to get a feel for the city."

"I did, and it's wonderful. Thank goodness you insisted I put on these sneakers."

"I don't even pack a pair of high heels," she said, peering down at her sandaled feet. "If my former modeling agent could see me in Birkenstocks, she'd cringe. I must look like a yokel in these clodhoppers." She self-consciously ran a hand through her hair.

"Not at all," I said. "You're far too beautiful for people to notice what's on your feet. And if they do, they'll simply consider it a new fashion statement."

"Aren't you a dear, Jessica. I wasn't really fishing for a compliment, but you gave me a lovely one anyway."

Olga and I had had a leisurely brunch at home— Vaughan had gone off early for a tennis game—after which she had trotted me around to some her favorite places. We'd stopped at a bakery to pick up *bolillos,* a kind of Mexican hard roll. Then she pulled me into a bookstore to see if they stocked my mysteries in Spanish or English. They did. In both languages. We admired the artwork in the windows of several galleries, one of which handled Olga's favorite artist, Sarah Christopher, the creator of the colorful oil paintings hanging in her home. And we purchased postcards to send off to New York and Cabot Cove. It seemed to me we'd made a big circle before climbing uphill to the square.

The day was warm but not uncomfortable. Olga wore a flower-patterned wrap dress that emphasized her long, slim body. She'd tossed a cashmere cardigan over her shoulders, tying the sleeves in front like a scarf. I had on my favorite lightweight pantsuit, the soft taupe one that refuses to wrinkle, and the gym shoes Olga had pressed me to wear: "I don't want you twisting an ankle your first day out." After negotiating the cobblestone streets—the sidewalks were too narrow to walk two abreast comfortably—I was happy that I'd followed her suggestion.

"I hope I haven't worn you out."

"Not me. I'm the original trouper. I love a good long walk."

"Well, you're in the right place now. Living in New York, we've gotten used to doing without a car. Having one here would be more of a burden than a convenience. There's nowhere to put it."

"I noticed the house doesn't have a garage."

"Parking space is at a premium, but honestly, everything we need is within easy walking distance."

"You don't have to convince me," I said. "I've been managing without a car my entire life."

"So you have. Of course, it's handy to have one from time to time, but if we want to explore a bit farther out, we can take a taxi, or one of our new friends will give us a lift. Everyone is so welcoming. We already have a wide group of friends down here. You'll meet more of them later."

Our walk ended in front of the police station, where we ran into a large, bushy-haired man with a broad grin on his face coming out of the building. Behind him was a stocky young man wearing a Che Guevara T-shirt. He appeared to be in his early twenties.

"Well, if it isn't the gorgeous Mrs. Buckley. Fancy meeting you here, of all places." His booming voice had people on the street turning to see who he was. The young man turned his back and pretended not to know him.

Olga cringed. "Hello, Woody," she said, her voice distinctly lacking in enthusiasm.

"How's the great white hunter? Ready for a little adventure?"

Olga ignored his questions. "Jessica, this is Woody Manheim and his son, Philip."

Woody frowned. "Boy, turn around and say hello."

"I'm not a boy, Dad."

"Then act like a man. Don't embarrass me."

Olga interrupted the scolding. "Woody, this is our guest, Jessica Fletcher."

Woody's face lit up. "Sure, sure, I recognize you," he said, pumping my hand. "Saw you on the *Today* show.

Pleased to make your acquaintance. How's that Katie Couric? Is she as nice as she seems on TV?"

I assured him she was.

"Pretty thing. Can't compare to our beauty queen here, though, can she?"

"Dad," Philip said with a groan.

"Woody, could you lower your voice, please?" Olga said in a hoarse whisper.

"Sorry. Was I shouting?"

Olga nodded, pulling the sleeves of her sweater closer.

"You're impossible," Philip said with disgust. "I'm outta here." He walked away without acknowledging Olga or me.

"Kids!" Woody winked at me and shrugged. "Hearing's not what it used to be," he said, making an exaggerated effort to speak more softly.

I had a feeling Woody had been loud all his life regardless of the state of his hearing.

"I never met a real live celebrity before," he said. "Not much of a reader. You know how it is—so much to do, so little time. But you looked great on TV."

Olga was tall, but Woody towered over her. Broad in the shoulders, the waist, and the hips, he would have been intimidating but for the pleasant expression on his face. Evidently, he greeted everyone with the same hail-fellow-well-met gusto, and it was hard not to smile back, although I don't think his son would have agreed with my assessment.

"Jessica, don't let us keep you," Olga said. "I'll meet you over there when you're through giving your police report."

She pointed to an ice cream stand on the corner of the park.

"Nice to have met you," I said to Woody.

"Oh, I'll see you later at the beauty queen's party." He cut a glance at Olga and guffawed.

"Woody, may I talk to you a moment?" she said, leading him away.

There was no door to the station house, only an arched opening leading to a flight of stairs. As I mounted the first step, men in brown uniforms, carrying rifles and with bandoliers crisscrossing their chests, clattered down the staircase. I flattened myself against the cool wall to keep out of their way, but there seemed to be unending numbers of them.

"Señora, Señora, this is not a good place to stand," said a voice to my side.

"My apologies," I said to a stern-faced a man in a loose-fitting white shirt and a baseball cap. "However, I have an appointment with . . ." I held up the card provided by the officers who had rescued Juanito and me. "I'm to see Javier Rivera. I understand his office is up there." I nodded toward the second floor. "Do you know him?"

"I do. Let me assist you." He pushed past me, shouted something in Spanish, and the crowd of men stopped where they were and squeezed to the right to allow us to pass. We climbed quickly but faced a new squad at the top of the stairs, and my escort had to repeat his instructions so we could enter the hall. Once we were safely on the next level, the stairwell filled again with descending men.

"Soldiers," he called over his shoulder. He led me past a

series of offices and a huge magnetic board showing the police duty roster, with silver disks to represent officers and crisscrossing rows indicating shift times and areas of the patrols. It hung next to a map of the city marked with colored pins. At the end of the hall, he drew a ring of keys out of his pocket to unlock a door on which a sign read, EL JEFE DE POLICÍA. "Have a seat," he said once we were inside. He hung his ball cap on a hook on the wall, revealing a salt-and-pepper crew cut, took the chair behind the desk, and dropped the keys into a drawer.

"Are you the chief of police?"

"Javier Rivera at your service," he said. "Don't look so surprised." He caught my glance at his clothes and shrugged. "I'm usually more formal, but my son is playing baseball this afternoon and I'm leaving here"—he squinted at his watch—"in an hour. So whatever it is, make it quick."

"I won't keep you long," I said. "I'm a little surprised to be reporting to someone as important as the chief of police. Is this standard procedure?"

"For the moment. My second and I are the only ones on the squad who speak intelligible English. Others say they speak the language, but you couldn't tell it by me. Since the city has a sizable English-speaking population, we need to be able to communicate clearly. We're setting up lessons for the officers, but it'll be a while before that bears any fruit." He sighed. "So tell me. Why are you here?"

"My driver and I were on the road from León to San Miguel when a ban—when a thief waylaid our car, took our money and some of my jewelry, and ran off."

51

"A *bandido,* you were going to say. A familiar story." He pulled out a blank form from a pile of papers on his desk and handed it to me along with a pen. "What time of the day was this?"

"Didn't your officers give you a summary?"

"I'll ask the questions. What time of day was this?"

"Actually, it was at night. I'd say around one or two in the morning."

He tipped his chin down, raised his brow, and peered up at me through thick black lashes. "Don't you know better than to travel at night in Mexico? You should be grateful you weren't shot, or worse. That was a very bad decision, Mrs. . . ? I didn't catch your name."

"Fletcher. Jessica Fletcher. Yes, Chief, I understand that, but my flight was delayed, and the person who was supposed to pick me up at the airport—"

"No excuses," he said, interrupting. "There's no good reason to be driving around these roads in the dark. You appear to be an intelligent woman. You must have heard about crime in Mexico. Stories like this have been printed in every paper in the world. Tourism is down all over the country as a result. Why didn't you just stay in a hotel overnight?"

"I was told the hotels in León were all filled."

"They always say that, but if you'd gone to one, they would have found you something, even if they'd had to kick one of their staff out of bed. Who drove you, then, if your original driver never showed?"

"The son of one of the men who worked at the airport."

I felt foolish as soon as the words were out of my mouth. I knew he was going to pounce on that. I had taken a risk by trusting Juanito, but I'd thought it was a small one. That his father had awakened him at midnight to drive a stranded stranger struck me as a generous act, not a nefarious one. Still, I had given Chief Rivera something else to seize upon, another reason to scold me. I headed him off. "Now, I know what you're about to say, but there you're wrong. Juanito was not in league with the *bandido*. I'd bet my life on that."

"Which was exactly what you did," he barked.

"Please let me finish. He was a very reliable young man who watched out for me as best he could. In fact, he was very protective."

"Driving a brand-new car, no doubt, with seat belts and air bags. Hmmm?"

"That's an entirely different matter."

A small smirk came and went on his lips. He waved at the form in my hands. "Just fill that out and we'll see what we can do, but I have to inform you that we never find stolen articles. Whatever this guy took has probably been fenced three times by now. And the thief himself is likely to be miles away."

"I wasn't expecting that you would recover my belongings. But it might be helpful to you to have a description of the robber. Do you do any investigation at all, or am I wasting my time?"

"Now don't get your back up. We'll check into it. Just stating the facts."

"I wonder if could ask you a question?"

His eyes were wary. "Sure."

"How did you know to address me in English when I was downstairs?"

"Easy. First of all, we have a very big expat community down here, which you must have noticed by now. Half of them are across the street in the park. Americans and Canadians are retiring here by the dozens. You're blond, wearing a brand-new pair of Nikes, and a carrying a handbag that wasn't made in Mexico. Plus, you weren't afraid to buck the tide of uniforms—a very American attitude—and you were trying to get into a police station, not out of it."

"Interesting. Do you mind if I ask you another?"

"Shoot."

"When did you leave New York?"

He snorted. "How'd you figure that one out?"

"Let's leave aside your brashness for the moment."

"What you really mean is rudeness."

"Yes, well, you speak English with a New York accent. I used to live in New York City, so the sound of New Yorkers is not unknown to me."

"No kidding. Where?"

"In Manhattan."

"What were you doing there? You don't sound like a native New Yorker to me."

"I was teaching at Manhattan University."

"Interesting. Where did you live?"

"I had an apartment at Penfield House."

"Nice address," he said.

"Nice way to change the subject."

The smirk appeared again.

"If your accent were not enough," I said, "your New York Yankees baseball cap over there was a sure giveaway."

"Doesn't mean a thing. A lot of people are Yankees fans."

"Not where I come from."

"Where's that?"

"Cabot Cove, Maine."

"Maine? They don't even have a baseball team."

"Not a major league one. But Boston's not too far away. And they do."

"Who are you talking about? The Red Sox? No comparison. Not even close. Shouldn't even say their name in the same breath as the Yankees."

"When I left New York yesterday ..." I paused. *My goodness, was it only yesterday?* I thought. *So much has happened.* "When I left New York, if I'm not mistaken—and I don't believe I am—Boston had a three-game lead in a four-game series." I smiled in triumph. "You can look it up if you don't believe me. It'll be on the Internet."

Chief Rivera's smirk faded. "They'll make it up. It's still early in the season. The Yankees have depth. They always come out on top." He scowled at me. "Now who's changing the subject?"

I nodded. "What did you do in New York, Chief? Were you a policeman there, too?"

His face relaxed. "Twenty years with NYPD."

"I'll bet speaking Spanish was a real help to you as a policeman in New York."

"In the Latino neighborhoods. I speak Spanish with a Mexican accent, but I can put on a Puerto Rican, Dominican, or even Cuban accent when I need to."

"How did you find a job down here?"

His expression became contemplative. "When I retired from the force, I couldn't take the quiet. I was used to the action, you know?"

I nodded.

"The wife got disgusted, divorced me, and moved upstate with the kids. They're in college now. I bounced around for a while. Then I read about a job opening in Mexico."

"And you already knew the language."

"Not only that. I knew the area, too. My parents were from Guanajuato originally. We used to come back for a family visit every couple of years. Anyway, at the time Mexico was hiring cops by the dozen to combat the increase in crime. When the tourists started avoiding the resorts, the government knew they'd better do something, and fast. I guess they must've run out of local talent and gave me a shot at it. But it's no big deal in San Miguel. It's relatively safe."

I raised my eyebrows. Not in my experience, it wasn't.

He noted my expression. "Well, there are always exceptions, but San Miguel is no Mexico City."

"And you wish it were?"

"Not really. But I wouldn't mind putting some time in in the big city. I don't think there's much of a chance of that. My wife, the new one, that is—I met her down here— she'd kill me if I even suggested it. It's her little boy, my stepson, I'm taking to play baseball."

"And I'm keeping you. I'll fill this out right now." I picked up the pen and started writing quickly. "Were you made police chief right away?" I asked as I recorded the details from the night before.

"No, not at first. But my predecessor got caught with his hand in the till, so to speak. He was moonlighting as a *bandido*."

I raised my head, startled.

"I guess the local officials decided a guy from Spanish Harlem wouldn't have the illegal connections down here, and so they promoted me into the job."

"And you've cleaned up Dodge City."

"Workin' on it."

"Is it common for the military to share office space with the police in Mexico?" I asked.

"You mean the soldiers?"

"I was surprised to see them here."

"The federal government is big on cooperative efforts, partly so they can get a handle on criminal issues. The army is everywhere. But it also means having troops in place if needed."

"What might they be needed for?"

"Tons of stuff. The drug trade is always a concern, plus illegal immigration and revolutionary groups."

"I didn't realize there were any revolutionary groups in this area."

"Most of them are in the south, but there are little pockets all over the country. The local ones call themselves the Revolutionary Guanajuato Brigade. They've been operating in this area for around fifteen years. Probably three guys with a copy machine. They specialize in statements to the press, but that's about it. I haven't seen any evidence of paramilitary operations, but if the administration wants a show of federal strength, that's fine with me."

There was a sharp rap on the door, and a tall, muscular man poked his head in. "Jefe?"

"C'mon in. We got another *bandido* victim here. Mrs. Fletcher, this is Captain Ignacio Gutierrez, my second in command."

"*Complació para encontrarlo,*" he said, barely sparing me a glance.

The chief frowned. "You take care of it," he said in English, "since you got your eyes on my job."

Gutierrez grunted and backed out of the room.

There was an awkward moment of silence. I bent my head to complete the questions on the form, which were in both languages.

"Here you go," I said, giving it back to him. "It's just a brief summary of my encounter with the robber. If I think of anything else, may I give you a call?"

He scanned the account, holding the sheet in one hand as the other groped on the desk for a business card. "Brief, huh?" he said, as his hand landed on a tray of cards and extracted one. "I see he wore a plaid *paliacate.*"

"I beg your pardon?" I said, as I took the card he extended to me.

"Kerchief. You're sure it was *plaid*?"

"It was dark, but I'm pretty sure it was plaid."

"This kind of stuff doesn't mean a thing," he said, dropping my form on his desk with a flip of his hand. "Everyone and his brother wears a kerchief down here. Same with the cowboy sombrero."

"I was just trying to be accurate."

"The coughing, now that's new. Never heard of a *bandido* with the flu before."

"It might be pneumonia or tuberculosis."

His brows rose. "It might."

"I'm glad I've given you something to go on," I said with a straight face.

His gaze was piercing. "Can't tell whether you're kidding or being serious."

"I think I'll let you figure that out," I said, rising. "You've got a baseball game to get to."

He stood up and grabbed his Yankees cap. "I'll walk you out." He patted his pockets, pushed aside some papers on his desk, and looked under a book.

"Top drawer on the right," I said.

"Huh?"

"Your keys. I saw you put them in the top drawer on the right."

"Oh, yeah?" He narrowed his eyes at me, opened the drawer, pulled out the keys, and stuffed them in his trouser pocket. "Let's go."

He put his cap on when we reached the sidewalk in front of the building. "Nice meeting you, Mrs. Fletcher. Stay out of more trouble while you're here."

"I hope to," I said.

"By the way, I forgot to ask what you taught at Manhattan University. What was it? English? History? You look like an English professor to me. Am I right?"

"I did teach English at one time."

"I knew it."

"But that was on the secondary level."

"Oh." Disappointment crossed his face.

"No, Chief. When I taught at Manhattan University, it wasn't English."

"What was it, then?"

"It was criminology." I managed to smother my smile until I was across the street and heading toward the corner where I was to meet Olga. But I enjoyed having surprised him, and as I walked away I pictured the expression that must have been on his face.

Chapter Seven

"I arrived in the middle of the night, so I hadn't had an opportunity to see what the house looked like from the outside. It was quite a surprise this morning."

"It's a modest-looking street, Jessica, but behind those rough walls are some of the most elegant homes in San Miguel, and right up the block is the one of the best small hotels in the world, Casa de Sierra Nevada."

"I think we passed it this afternoon on the way to El Jardin."

"You must let Olga and Vaughan treat you to dinner there. The food is out of this world."

"Perhaps I can make it my treat instead, Cathie. I was hoping to take them out as a thank-you for hosting me."

"That's the perfect place. I happen to know they love it."

Cathie Harrison was one of the guests at a gathering the Buckleys had arranged to welcome me. A pretty blond lady, she and her husband, Eric Gewirtz, and their son, Robbie, were spending the summer in San Miguel, while their daughter, Jena, took classes at the Universidad del Valle de Mexico. "We're all learning Spanish together," she said, "but Eric couldn't resist bringing a basketball with him. He coaches the game at home. He and Jena have even gotten up a team with some of the local students. That's where they are right now, playing basketball. I hope they make it here before the party is over."

"I'll look forward to meeting them," I said. "I understand Eric helped Vaughan set up his media room."

"The 'boys' toys,' I call them. They like to surf the Internet on a huge screen, play music too loud for anyone's comfort, and watch European sports on the satellite dish even though they have no idea what the rules of the games are."

I laughed. "Is that what they do?"

"I'm convinced of it."

"Excuse me, Cathie," Olga said, taking my arm. "May I pull Jessica away? I have some people who are dying to meet her."

Olga escorted me to the other end of the stone-tiled courtyard. It was a square space, enclosed on all four sides by the two-story stucco structure that was the Buckleys' home. Two tall carved doors that marked the main entrance to the house were flanked by long windows, their rust-colored shutters thrown open against the pale yellow walls. A small balcony, red flowers dangling from boxes affixed to its wrought iron railing, jutted out above the entry. On the opposite side of the courtyard, a short passageway ended in the heavy wooden door leading to the street. To the right of the exit was a wall fountain, a brightly painted ceramic face with water spewing from its mouth into a semicircular basin covered in mosaic tile. To the left, an acacia tree gracefully shaded the corner, as well as several of the myriad tropical plants that grew in terra-cotta pots of various sizes strategically placed to give the impression of a lush landscape. The patio was spacious and elegant, ideal for entertaining, and Olga had filled it with her friends and neighbors for a cocktail party in my honor. We greeted them as I squeezed through the crowd trying to keep up with her.

"So nice to meet you, Jessica."

"Nice to meet you, too."

"Jessica Fletcher! How exciting. Is this your first trip to Mexico?"

"It's my first trip to San Miguel."

"I've read every one of your books, Mrs. Fletcher. Would you mind if I brought one by for you to autograph?"

"I'd be delighted, but call me Jessica, please."

"Hello. We wondered if you were here. Welcome to SMA."

"SMA?"

"San Miguel de Allende."

"Thank you. It's a pleasure to be here."

"Oh, you must meet Roberto. He's a writer, too."

"Is he here?"

"Heard about your introduction to Mexico last night. Sorry about that."

"That's kind of you to say, but no real harm done."

"Great party, Olga."

"Stay a while. There's a mariachi band coming later."

"She's a wonderful hostess, isn't she?"

"Who's the caterer, dear?"

"A company called Who's Cooking. I'll give you their card."

"It's J. B. Fletcher, isn't it?"

"That's right."

"Nice meeting you."

Olga drew to a halt just before a colonnade that ran along one side of the building and provided shelter from the sun. Under the arched ceiling, and to the right of a pair of open French doors leading to the kitchen, was a series of rattan chairs and sofas on which guests lounged and helped themselves to hors d'oeuvres and rainbow-colored cocktails offered by Maria Elena and a couple hired for the occasion. As she delivered the new drinks, Maria Elena removed the empty glasses and placed clean napkins on the glass top of the low table in front of the guests.

Olga turned her back to the group and pretended to show me a miniature date palm. "The couple on the sofa are Dina and Roberto Fisher," she said softly. " 'Roberto' used to be plain 'Robert' back home. His wife still slips occasionally and calls him Bob. I'm told he sold his pharmacy to some big chain and they've been living on the profits. He's taken on a whole new persona down here. One or two of his treatises on Mexican culture appeared in some obscure academic publication, so he now considers himself a published author. Would you mind terribly talking with him?"

"Not at all. Why would you even ask?"

She sighed heavily. "Because he says his next project is to write a murder mystery. Vaughan saw a few pages of the latest attempt and told Roberto that they were awful."

"Really?" I said. "Vaughan's usually so diplomatic."

She sighed. "Not this time, I'm afraid. Roberto gets under his skin. He accused Vaughan of being jaded, said that someone with sensitivity would understand what he's trying to do. As you can imagine, things have been a bit tense between them."

"I'm surprised you invited them."

"I'm trying to smooth things over. We're only here a short time and it's a small community. Roberto and Dina have a lot of friends. I don't want us to create a division where there was none."

"That's wise of you. Does Vaughan agree?"

"He's promised to behave, and he knows I'll hold him to it."

"How can I help?"

"I realize it's an imposition, but Roberto has talked of nothing but Jessica Fletcher since he heard you were coming. I hope you won't hate me for putting you together."

"Don't give it a second thought, Olga. I meet many would-be mystery writers in my travels, and I'll be happy to talk shop with him."

"You'll have my undying gratitude, and his wife's, too, I'm sure."

"I've always wanted your undying gratitude. Lead me to him."

We turned back toward the colonnade and went through an arch into the shaded passage, where Vaughan was talking with several of the guests. He rose when he saw us and held a chair for me. "Ah, the guest of honor. Ladies and gentlemen, my friend and colleague Jessica Fletcher. Let me introduce you around, Jessica. This handsome couple is Roberto and Dina Fisher, longtime residents of San Miguel, although originally from . . . Detroit, was it?"

"Correct, Señor." Roberto was a small man with a pencil-thin mustache and suspiciously dark hair for his age, which I judged to be his sixties. He held a green drink in his hand and was dressed in a blue version of the same type of traditional Mexican shirt the police chief had been wearing earlier. I dredged up the name, guayabera, from memories of my last visit south of the border many years ago. Short-sleeved, it had a pleated front and four pockets and was worn outside the trousers. His wife was also dressed in Mexican attire—a white cotton blouse and skirt with hand-embroidered flower motifs at the collar, waist, and hem. She wore her silver hair pulled into a chignon.

Roberto put his drink down on the cocktail table and got up from the sofa to shake my hand; his wife waved from her seat. "My husband is a writer, too," she trilled.

"You are?" I said, greeting him. "Well, we must compare notes sometime."

"I'll look forward to it," Roberto said with a satisfied grin. He sat again, nudged his wife, and shot Vaughan a now-we'll-see look.

"This lovely lady, Jessica," Vaughan continued, "is responsible for the paintings you've been admiring in our house. Sarah Christopher."

"What a pleasure to meet such a talented artist," I said. "I'm enjoying your work."

"You must come visit my studio sometime," she replied.

"It would be my pleasure."

"And that gentleman is former major Woody Manheim, late of the US Army, whom I understand you encountered this afternoon."

"Please don't get up," I said. "Nice to see you again, Mr. Manheim."

"It's Woody, my dear," he said, raising his glass to me. "We're all very informal down here. Can I call you Jessica?"

"Please do."

"May I get you a drink?" Woody asked. "The bartender makes a mean margarita."

"Thank you, no," I said. "Later, perhaps."

"We were just talking about our plans for the next few days, Jessica," Vaughan said. "Woody and I are going on the mail run."

"Oh, yes, you mentioned that last night."

"This is where I make my exit," said Olga, who'd been observing the introductions. "I have to check on the caterers." She gave her husband a stern glance and walked away.

"The wife's not too happy about this, is she?" Woody said.

"She's just worried about us," Vaughan said.

"And all your assurances of our safety have gone right over her pretty head, is that it?"

"Something like that, Woody."

"I've been doing it for close to three years now," Woody said proudly. "Never been stopped. Had a few close calls, though," he said, chuckling. "I could tell you some stories." His expression sobered. "But I never told Olga about those."

"I think she may have heard about them anyway," Vaughan said.

"What is the mail run, if you don't mind my asking?" I said.

"They're driving up to Laredo to pick up mail for those who have post office boxes there," Sarah Christopher said. She was a sturdy woman in her thirties, or maybe early forties, with dark brown eyes, soft cocoa-colored skin, and thick black hair worn in a cloud of curls around her face. "Some people don't trust the Mexican postal service. I for one."

"Why's that?" I asked.

"Because important mail doesn't always make it here. Between the corrupt government, customs, and the postal workers, you're lucky if anything gets through," she said. "I had a box of paint confiscated once. I don't know what they thought might be in the tubes. Drugs are smuggled out of this country, not into it." She gestured with her hands and I noticed she had blue stains on her fingers. "I had to fill in reams of forms, and when the new order finally arrived almost a year later, the local post office wanted to charge me the equivalent of five hundred dollars in duty. For a set costing half that amount. I'll never do that again."

"My heavens," I said. "I can understand why you were upset."

"I don't bother with MexPost anymore," she said. "If Vaughan picks up a package for me in Texas, the border guards will barely give it a glance. He's got that honest face." She gave Vaughan a wink and a smile. He shifted uncomfortably in his seat and cleared his throat.

"A lot of retirees, like me, don't want their pension or Social Security checks going through Mexico City before they get here," Woody added. "They tend to disappear, and it's the devil to get a replacement. Much simpler to have them mailed to an address in the States."

"From what I've heard, a letter from the U.S. can take three weeks or six months to arrive, Jessica," Vaughan added.

"And you'd better not forget to tip the mailman on Postman's Day or you may *never* see it," Sarah said.

"When is that, anyway?" Vaughan asked.

"November," Roberto said. "But I give my guy a little extra more often. You've got to know when to tip. That's the way to get good service in Mexico."

"There's no such thing as far as I'm concerned," Sarah said. "Everyone has his hand out. If they were paid a decent wage to begin with, then maybe you'd get good service. Anyway, Vaughan, you don't stay in San Miguel long enough to wait for something to be delivered by MexPost."

"You can always use FedEx or UPS," Roberto put in.

"*You* can use them," Woody said. "It costs a fortune from here."

"What's it going to cost *you* in gas and tolls?"

"We're amortizing the cost over more than twenty families with P.O. boxes. It doesn't amount to much."

"If you ask me, it's just an excuse to get away for a few days," Roberto said. "I've been here fourteen years and I get my mail just fine."

"We don't get much mail, dear," his wife reminded him.

"We get a postcard from your brother every now and then."

"Only when he's traveling. Otherwise he calls us on his cell phone."

"Well, we get other mail."

"I'm looking forward to the trip," Vaughan said. "Kind of like being with the Pony Express, riding across the range to deliver the mail. Besides, I had my secretary open a post office box for me in Laredo. There should be a manuscript waiting, and I don't want to miss that."

His companions laughed. "Didn't take you long to learn the way of things," Woody said. "Reminds me of a story when I was stationed at Fort Bliss."

"No, Woody, spare us," Sarah said in mock dramatic fashion, the back of her hand on her brow.

"Well, if you don't want to hear it . . ." He was clearly offended.

"Save it for tomorrow," Vaughan said. "We're going to need stories to entertain each other on the long ride, and telling them will keep you awake. I don't want you falling asleep at the wheel."

"Aren't you going to spell him with the driving?" I asked Vaughan.

"He can't drive my car," Woody said.

"Does he need a Mexican driver's license?"

"It's not as easy as that. It's the Mexican laws. They don't want anyone outside your family driving your car. If we got caught with Vaughan driving, they'd take my car away. Permanently."

"That's awful," I said.

"It would be no loss with that old junker you have. Did you get the radio fixed yet?" Sarah asked Woody.

"I'll have you know that junker, as you call it, has over a hundred thousand miles and still gets twenty miles to the gallon. It's in great shape—no rust, tires are good, engine's completely rebuilt. There's just a few little quirks, like the radio."

"I rest my case," she said, rising and waving at us. "I'm going to get some dinner. Vaughan? Join me?"

Vaughan got to his feet. "Thanks. I'm not hungry right now. I'll have something later," he said.

Sarah looped her index finger in the gap between buttons on Vaughan's shirt. "I'll just have to find you later," she said. "I'm hungry now."

It was the first time I'd ever seen Vaughan blush. He was always cool and in control, but evidently Sarah's brazen flirting made him uneasy.

"My gallery opening is in three days," she said. "Actually three nights. I hope you'll be home in time for it, but if not, you can come to my studio and I'll show you what you missed."

Vaughan cleared his throat. "I'm not sure of our schedule," he said, "but in any case Woody and I have to check out his vehicle before we take off. Right, Woody? Would you all excuse us, please."

Woody took the hint and lumbered out of his chair.

"I take it they're not an item anymore?" Roberto said when the others left.

"Woody didn't show up at her last opening, so she dumped him," Dina said. "She's too young for him anyway."

"Why don't we follow Sarah to the buffet?" I said. "We can come back and talk over dinner."

While we'd been chatting, the caterers had set up tables across from the colonnade. The Fishers took plates and joined the line that had formed, and I fell in behind them. The guests at the party were a convivial group, chatting and laughing in knots of three or four. Most of the men wore guayaberas, like Roberto's, and the women were casually elegant, except for obvious displays of jewelry. For the most part they appeared to be members of the expatriate community—conversation was in English—but I was happy to see that here and there were some faces that reflected the Mexican population.

It struck me as strange that people would move to a foreign country and make no effort to become part of the greater community, shunning the local residents and instead forging a miniature version of what they'd left at home. What I enjoy most about visiting a country—or any new place, for that matter—is meeting the people, learning about the culture, and participating in a society different from my own. I knew Vaughan and Olga felt the same way.

Roberto turned to wave at a gentleman behind me. "Haven't seen you in a while, Guy. Are you avoiding me?"

"Got better things to do than keep track of where you are," the man replied, frowning. "But now that I see you, I've got a great tip for you."

"Your last tip cost too much. I sold it at a loss."

"That was your second mistake," the man said. "By this time next year, that baby will be through the roof."

"And I suppose I have to ask what my first mistake was?" Roberto said, his annoyance apparent.

"That's Guy Kovach," Dina whispered to me. "Unbelievably rich. He throws money around like rice at a wedding. His wife, Nancy, is always dripping in diamonds." Her voice held a combination of disdain and awe. "He's a big-time stockbroker from New York."

I nodded but was taken aback. The man under discussion would never have passed muster in a staid Wall Street firm. He was heavyset, with a florid face and wavy brown hair. He wore a gold chain around his neck, gold bracelets on both wrists, and on his thick fingers were several rings, one with a large diamond set in it. If we hadn't been in central Mexico, I wouldn't have been surprised to learn he was wheeling and dealing in a Las Vegas casino.

"You didn't buy that stock through me," Kovach said, pointing a thick finger at Roberto. "You thought you'd sneak around and get it on the Internet and avoid paying my broker's fee, didn't you? Well, your cheapness backfired. You get what you pay for, Fisher. Remember that."

"I make plenty of money without your tips."

"Glad to hear it," Kovach said, grinning. "We'll do business yet." He left the line and walked to the other end of the buffet table.

The Fishers and I filled our plates from the wonderful-looking platters and took our seats under the colonnade, but without the rest of the group. I was disappointed to find that Sarah hadn't returned, nor had Vaughan or Woody.

Maria Elena emerged from the French doors and began clearing away the dishware and glasses that had been left on the low table. Roberto drained his glass and put it on her tray.

"Would you like another drink, Señor Fisher?"

"No, gracias. He tenido bastante."

"Señoras?"

"I'll have another piña colada," Dina said. "I'm not driving."

"Nothing for me, thanks," I said.

Maria Elena returned to the kitchen, and I heard her give directions to someone, presumably for Dina's drink.

A man's voice responded in an angry tone, and she replied in kind. He raised his voice a notch and she matched it.

"Are you enjoying San Miguel?" Dina asked, ignoring the argument.

"Very much," I replied. "Olga gave me a mini-tour

today. We walked everywhere. The house is so conveniently located."

"We don't live in town, but we have three acres."

"Three and a half," her husband said.

"Three and a half," she echoed.

The disagreement in the kitchen was getting louder, and I saw a few guests turn our way with curious expressions.

"What made you decide to move to Mexico from Detroit?" I asked.

"The good life," Roberto said.

"You can live very well down here for not a lot of money," Dina added. She looked to her husband for confirmation.

I heard shushing sounds from the kitchen. The angry combatants lowered their voices, but fragments of the squabble continued to be audible. "Excuse me," I said. "Let me find out if something is wrong."

"Don't bother. It's just a sibling spat," Roberto said.

"What do you mean?"

"Maria Elena is having a fight with her brother. Hector doesn't like taking orders from his sister."

" 'Course, it's a lot more expensive now than when we first came here," Dina mused, as if unaware of the controversy inside.

A man dressed in black stomped through the French doors. He whipped a white apron from his waist, rolled it into a ball, and flung it behind a miniature palm.

Maria Elena ran after him, retrieved the apron, and growled something through gritted teeth.

"She says he'll never work here again if she has any say about it," Roberto translated.

"Oh, dear," I said. "And Vaughan spoke so highly of him."

"The Latin temperament heats quickly, but it cools quickly, too," Roberto said. "They'll forget about it tomorrow."

Dina forged ahead. "Inflation is going up, eroding the dollar, not to mention that the place has become far too popular," she said. "Roberto always says there are too many expats now."

"That's true," her husband said, reentering the conversation. "Loads of Americans and Canadians. I liked it better when we had more of the place to ourselves."

I didn't remind him that he was an expatriate himself.

"You're thinking I'm an expat, too, and shouldn't talk."

I laughed. "Guilty as charged," I said.

"Well, it's true. What attracted me to Mexico was that it was exotic. I wanted to immerse myself in its culture. The newcomers are different. They don't even bother to learn Spanish—maybe a word or two, but that's all. Look around you. I'll bet half the people here can't speak any Spanish."

"I was thinking the same thing only a little while ago," I said.

"They know how to ask for the bathroom," his wife said, giggling.

Roberto shot her an irritated look and she lowered her head, then raised it and looked around. "I wonder where my drink is."

"Many of the expats operate shops here," Roberto continued, "and a lot of the locals speak English, too. The new-comers can deal with English speakers every day. There's even an English-language newspaper."

"*Noticias*," Dina said.

"I beg your pardon."

"*Noticias*. That's the name of the newspaper in English," he said

"Oh. I take it you speak Spanish well?"

"Fluently," Roberto replied. "They tell me I sound like I was born here. Of course, that may be a little flattery, but I get by very well."

"Not me," Dina added. "I barely know a word."

"Not 'I,' you mean," he said.

"Not I," she said. "Bob took lessons . . . I mean, Roberto took Spanish for two years before we moved here, and he still takes classes from time to time."

"You must be a quick study," I said.

"Gotta be able to converse with the locals. Only way to get along if you live here. I didn't move to Mexico to surround myself with Americans. You've got to work on it." He frowned at his wife, who was craning her neck to look into the kitchen.

"It must have been very difficult to make such a big change in your life," I said.

"Not if you approach it methodically. I've conducted a detailed study of the Mexican culture," he said. "And I've written extensively about my findings. I'd be honored if you'd read some of it while you're here and give me your thoughts."

"That would be very nice," I said.

"Roberto is a scholar," his wife added, turning to face me.

"Yes, in fact, I've had two articles accepted for publication by the *Reddington Journal of Mexican History and Culture.*"

"It's very exclusive," Dina said. "You know it, of course."

"I'm afraid I'm not familiar with that particular publication," I said.

"Oh, I was hoping you were. We haven't seen it yet, but they cashed the check and wrote a very nice letter," she said.

They cashed the check? It sounded as though Roberto had paid them to publish his articles.

"They're coming out in the fall," he said, "but you don't have to wait that long. I sent Vaughan a copy. He probably threw it on his bookshelf somewhere. He doesn't care for my writing. But I'm not discouraged. 'It is a rough road that leads to the heights of greatness.' The philosopher Seneca said that."

"In his *Epistles,*" I said, surprising myself that I remembered.

"Oh, here's my drink," Dina said, as Maria Elena placed a tall glass in front of her. The white concoction was topped with a piece of pineapple and a maraschino cherry.

Maria Elena laid a straw on the table next to it. *"Lo siento que tomó tan largo,"* she whispered.

"That's okay," Dina said. "It didn't take that long." She plucked off the piece of pineapple that had been balanced on the rim and popped it in her mouth.

"No offense," Roberto said to me. "I know he's your

friend. But Vaughan is more interested in the business of making money than in intellectual ideas."

I knew Olga wanted me to make the Fishers feel at ease, but I couldn't let his comment pass. "I think you're mistaken," I said. "Vaughan Buckley is one of the best-read men I know. He's knowledgeable in a wide variety of subjects, and he loves politics and poetry, biography, science, and everything in between."

That included, I was sure, "intellectual ideas," and very likely the Roman philosopher Roberto had just quoted. But I didn't say that. Roberto Fisher was evidently a man very taken with himself. I understood now why Olga was so hesitant to introduce me to him.

I felt a headache coming on. The conversation had been difficult, what with the argument in the kitchen between Maria Elena and her brother and the odd way Dina seemed to bounce in and out of the conversation, most of the time lost in whatever had been her last thought.

"I hear you're writing a murder mystery," I said to Roberto, hoping to lure him onto a safer topic.

"Yes. I'd like to pick your brain about that."

"Who gets killed and why?"

"I haven't figured that out yet, but it takes place in San Miguel. I know all the back streets and shady areas here, so I can really set the atmosphere."

Olga came up behind me and put her hands on my shoulders. "Did you people enjoy your meal?" she asked. "The Hoffmanns have just set out the desserts, so I hope no one's dieting."

"Who?" Roberto asked.

"The caterers, Donna and Alfred Hoffmann. They moved here recently and everyone is talking about how wonderful they are."

"Of course, the Hoffmanns."

Olga looped her arm in mine and pulled me to my feet. "Come along, now, Jessica. I insist you try their mango mousse. You don't mind, do you, Roberto? Dina? You'll have plenty of time to talk later."

"Sure," Roberto said. "You're going to be here for two weeks, right, Jessica? We'll have plenty of time to talk."

Two whole weeks! Well, at least the Fishers live out of town, I thought.

"I insist you come out and see our place," Dina said as we returned to the buffet.

I try not to have unkind thoughts, but I admit I was thinking at the moment, *Maybe Vaughan will let me come along with him and Woody on the mail run.*

Chapter Eight

The Buckleys' guest room was as comfortable as it was elegant, with a four-poster bed and crisp white linens. I slept very well the night after my first full day in San Miguel de Allende. The next morning, however, my rest was interrupted by the sound of voices raised in an argument. I tried not to eavesdrop, but Vaughan and Olga were in the hall outside my door.

"Don't you have any consideration for my feelings on this?"

"For godsakes, Olga, we've been over this a hundred times. I promised him I wouldn't cancel this time. I'm committed to going. I can't renege now. What kind of man gives his word and backs out at the eleventh hour?"

"A smart one."

"You want me to say I can't go because my wife's a nervous wreck and is nagging me to stay? That doesn't put *you* in a very nice light."

"If you need to use me as an excuse, go right ahead. Your life is more important than my reputation."

"Olga, sweetheart, I can't do that. And I'm not risking my life. I'm merely going for a drive."

"Don't try to snow me, Vaughan Buckley. I know all your tricks. You're going on an *adventure.* You said so yourself. I heard you compare this trip with the Pony Express. Aren't you a little old for adventures?"

"I'm not dead yet, thank you. And a little excitement never killed anyone."

"So you admit you're expecting something to happen."

"I admit no such thing."

"Is this to impress your girlfriend?"

"What are you saying?"

"You don't think I see how Sarah rolls her eyes at you. I may be farsighted, but I'm not blind. Is all of this to show her how *young* you really are?"

"Now you're being ridiculous. But I'm flattered that you're jealous."

"Don't change the topic."

"Me? You brought her up."

"Vaughan, be reasonable. Look what happened to Jessica, and she wasn't transporting bank drafts and checks and valuable packages. You'll be a sitting duck for any thug who knows the routine or keeps an eye on the border."

"You don't know what you're talking about. Woody has driven this route many, many times. He's even brought his son along at times. He's certainly not going to risk his flesh and blood."

"Let him take his son this time if it's so safe."

"The boy doesn't want to go, and I do."

"What about our time together? You could be stuck at the border for days, Vaughan."

"I'll make it up to you."

"And that's assuming they even let you back in the country with all that booty."

"We're not pirates carrying treasure. We're merely picking up the mail—letters, magazines, *bills,* most likely. And I'm hoping to collect a manuscript from a promising new author. It's nothing of value to anyone other than the recipients. There will be no problem getting back into Mexico. Woody says he knows all the border guards and they know him."

"Who says the border guards are honest?"

"Give the man a break. He spent thirty years in military intelligence. He knows which ones to trust."

"Vaughan, I've never asked you to sacrifice anything for me. I'm asking you, begging you, not to go. Tell Woody whatever you like. Make up a story. But please, don't take this trip."

"He's going to be here any moment, Olga, and my bag is already at the door."

Their voices faded as they walked downstairs.

The sun had barely peeked over the horizon. Even so, I'd been awake for a while, my circadian rhythms still on Eastern time. But I hadn't gotten out of bed, believing that if I lay still with my eyes closed, I might be lucky enough to drift off and catch another hour's sleep. However, circumstances conspired against me. With the reverberation of competing church bells, what sounded like a rooster crowing, and the Buckleys' quarrel, all hope of revisiting the land of Nod evaporated. I rose, showered, dressed quickly, and made my way downstairs to the kitchen.

Vaughan and Olga were seated at a table in front of open French doors that led to the colonnade and the courtyard beyond, where the stone pavers glowed pink in the early sunlight. The sound of birds chirping in the acacia tree provided background music to the lovely cool breeze that wafted inside. The beautiful morning was wasted on the Buckleys, who sipped their coffee in silence, each consumed with thoughts of the upcoming trip, and of each other.

Maria Elena bustled around the kitchen, stirring a pan of eggs and tomatoes on the stove and checking the toast she was baking in the oven. "Good morning, Señora. Breakfast will be ready in a few minutes. Would you like some coffee to start?"

"Good morning," I said. "Coffee would be wonderful."

"Good morning," Vaughan said, rising and forcing a smile.

"Oh, Jessica, did we wake you? I'm so sorry," Olga said, looking up from the newspaper that was folded on the table next to her cup.

"Not at all," I replied. "I'm still on New York time. It usually takes a day or so before I'm acclimated to a new schedule."

"Come, take my seat," Vaughan said. He held his chair for me. "I have to get something upstairs."

As he walked swiftly from the room, I reached over and squeezed Olga's hand. "He'll be fine," I said.

"Oh, Jessica, this is such a mistake. I'm just furious with him. A grown man going off on a lark, in a country he knows nothing about, where Americans are ripe pickings for criminals."

"Sometimes you have to let people make their own mistakes and learn from them. Vaughan is not a reckless man. He wouldn't intentionally put himself in danger."

Maria Elena slid plates of the eggs in front of us. "My brother, he has a gun, Señora Buckley. If you like, I can call him to come. He can ride with them for protection."

"*Muchas gracias,* Maria Elena, but I'm afraid that if I even so much as suggested such a thing, my husband would take my head off. I appreciate the offer, though." She shook her head. "If I had a gun myself," she muttered, "he'd never even get out of the house."

"How long is the ride to Laredo?" I asked.

She sighed and rolled her shoulders, trying to release the tension. "About thirteen or fourteen hours if you don't stop," she replied. "They'll probably be gone for at least three days, maybe more. Vaughan says they've booked a hotel in Monterrey for tonight, so they can get to the International Bridge first thing in the morning."

"Will they stay overnight in Laredo, too?"

"That depends. I heard Woody say something about having to register his car in the States again. Since they don't know how long that will take, it's possible they'll be stuck there longer."

"Things will go smoothly for them, I'm sure," I said, "and they'll be back here before you know it."

"This was supposed to be our vacation," she said. "Some vacation, with Vaughan away and me chewing my nails worrying about him. Am I crazy to feel this way? Tell me."

"I don't say you shouldn't worry about him, mind you. But if you and I plan something special for while he's away, we can make the time go quickly."

"I know I'm being selfish, Jessica. Vaughan was really looking forward to this trip and I've ruined it for him. But I can't help it. I have a horrible feeling something will go wrong."

"Have you ever had ESP before?"

"What do you mean?"

"Extrasensory perception."

"I know what the initials stand for," she said, her brow furrowing, then clearing as understanding dawned. "Oh, you mean have I ever worried about something and seen it come true?"

"Have you?"

She gave me a wry smile. "I can't say that I have."

"Well, that's a relief."

She laughed.

"I'm being silly, aren't I?"

"I wouldn't say that."

"Now I feel worse. I've made both of us miserable."

"Why don't you go wish Vaughan a safe trip? He'll feel better knowing that you'll be all right in his absence."

"I think I'll do that," she said, pushing back from the table. "Thank you, Jessica. You're very understanding. I'm sorry you have to put up with such a crybaby."

"Nonsense," I said, waving her away. "May I look at your newspaper?"

"Of course. We'll be right back."

"Take your time."

Maria Elena smiled at me as she cleared away Olga's untouched breakfast and put the plate in the oven to keep warm.

I had just turned to the editorial page when Woody came through the kitchen.

"Good morning," he said in a voice loud enough to chase the birds out of the tree. "Wonderful day for a road trip." He breathed in deeply and pounded his chest with a fist. "I love this weather. Perfect for driving. Of course, once we get out of the mountains, it'll heat up. But that's why it's good to get an early start. Nice chill in the air this morning."

"Good morning, Woody," I said. "Will you join me? Vaughan and Olga will be down soon."

"Don't mind if I do," he said, taking the chair Olga had abandoned. "Got some more of your wonderful coffee there, Maria?"

"*Buenos días, Señor Woody,*" Maria Elena said, bringing him a cup of steaming coffee. "Would you like some eggs?"

Woody assessed the food on my plate and nodded. "I've already eaten, but knowing what a good cook you are—you might give me just a little taste." He held his thumb and index finger an inch apart.

"*Solamente un momento*," she said, running to the stove and returning almost immediately with a plate of eggs and tomatoes for Woody.

"What kind of roads will you be traveling on?" I asked.

"Mostly highways. In fact"—he drew his wallet from his hip pocket and counted out some bills—"we're going to need money for the tolls, about thirty-five dollars' worth, I figure. I like to get that ready in advance." He folded the bills and tucked them in his breast pocket. "It's not a bad trip, just tedious," he said, digging into the eggs. "That's why I like to have someone along to help pass the time. Took my son once. What a mistake. The boy complained the whole way. I was ready to cut him off without a cent by the time we got back." He slurped some coffee and continued eating and talking. "Glad I picked Vaughan, though. Bet he's got a lot of stories he can tell about the book business. And he hasn't heard most of mine yet. Give me a new audience to practice on. Someone once told me I should write a book about my experiences. Maybe I can interest Buckley in publishing them. What do you think?"

I thought Vaughan might end up sorry that he had insisted on accompanying Woody, but I didn't say that. Instead, I said, "I've always thought there's a book in everyone. Stories about people are innately fascinating. But putting them into a readable form—that's the hard part."

"Yeah, well, if he likes the stories, can't he just find someone to write them up for me? You, for instance."

"Me?" I said. "That's kind of you to think of me, but I'm

much too busy writing my own stories to take on anyone else's."

"I was afraid you'd say that. I'm sure I can find someone," he said, shoveling in a forkful of eggs.

"Perhaps you will," I replied, concentrating on a piece of toast.

Vaughan and Olga returned with smiles on their faces. Vaughn had an arm draped around his wife's shoulder and she leaned against him.

"I'm ready to go and there you are, starting on breakfast," Vaughan said.

"Nope, nope," Woody said, leaning over the plate to finish the rest of his dish as he pushed up from the chair with his legs. "I'm ready." He swiped Olga's napkin over his lips. "All set," he said, taking a last gulp of coffee.

Outside, an old man and a burro plodded up the cobblestone street. The animal, whose muzzle was as white as his master's whiskers, carried a pair of panniers, straw baskets filled with red and green chiles, the sides stained with streaks the colors of the peppers. "*Buenos días, señoras, señores,*" he called out, touching the brim of his sombrero.

"*Buenos días,*" we replied.

We walked the men to the car, which Woody had left parked illegally on the street. It was an old station wagon, dirty but undented. It had probably been a bright blue when it was new, but even through the grime I could see that the color had faded over the years. The seats were covered in what looked like imitation curly sheepskin tied with strings that dangled down the back. A placard on a side window read NO HABLO ESPAÑOL. In the rear of the wagon, Woody had a series of cardboard cartons and plastic tubs with names printed on them in black marker. He grabbed Vaughan's small overnight bag, swung it into the backseat next to his own, and climbed behind the wheel.

Olga drew a white handkerchief with a crocheted edge from her pocket and pressed it into Vaughan's hand. "Something to remind you of me," she said.

Vaughan took the delicate scrap of cotton and traced the embroidered O on the corner with his thumb. He smiled at his wife. "You are *never* far from my thoughts, sweetheart. Thank you for understanding."

"Go now," she said, "before I have a change of heart."

Olga linked her arm with mine as Vaughan took the passenger seat. She blew him a kiss and tightened her grip on me as the engine roared to life and the men drove off, waving.

"Nancy Kovach told me Guy used to go on the mail run with Woody last year," she said, as the car rounded a corner and was gone from our sight. "She called herself 'a mail widow.' She said that's what she was for the days that they were gone. 'A mail widow.' I don't like that term."

"I don't either," I said as we turned back to the house. "I don't either."

Chapter Nine

Vaughan called from Monterrey that night.

"We're staying in a Best Western," he said. "It's clean and there's a bar nearby. That's all I care about. I want a nice big martini with my steak dinner. I deserve it."

Woody had reserved only one room to save on the cost, but Vaughan had threatened that his snoring would keep Woody up all night if each didn't have his own room. So they'd taken a second one, with Vaughan agreeing to cover the difference.

"But you don't snore," Olga said.

"Shhh. I don't want him to hear you."

"Is he right there?"

"No, we're just resting up before we find a place for dinner. But he can probably hear through walls. He certainly can talk through them."

Olga giggled.

"I had to get away," Vaughan said. "The man is a nonstop talker. He should have exhausted his vocal cords by now."

"And don't forget loud," Olga added. "I'm surprised you still have your hearing."

"I know everything there is to know about his military exploits, his failed marriage, his disappointing son, his buddies at the border, his love life . . ."

"He has a love life?"

"Yes. You didn't know about the attentive widows of San Miguel? Not to leave out a certain lady of artistic persuasion. You're not up on the local gossip, Olga."

"That's what I need you for. They all bare their souls to you so you'll publish them and make them famous."

"As a matter of fact, he's been pressuring me to put out a book of his stories, and he wants Jessica to write them for him."

"See? Your wife's brilliance shines again."

"Tell Jessica I may commit her to his project just to shut him up."

"If you do, don't complain to me when she wants a new publisher."

"Well, I'm paying the price for my need for adventure, sweetheart. I hope you're happy."

"I never wanted you to suffer, Vaughan. Well, maybe just a little."

"I'm suffering, just being away from you."

"Ahh. If that's the conclusion you draw after one day, I'm going to send you off on more trips."

"I love you."

"I love you, too, darling."

Olga replaced the phone in its cradle with a smile.

After Woody and Vaughan had left that morning, we'd spent the remainder of the day exorcising her demons in the spa at Casa de Sierra Nevada, the cosmopolitan little hotel only a short walk from the house. Between the full-body massage, the facial, the manicure, and the pedicure, there was not a place on our bodies that had not been pummeled into submission, kneaded till it cried uncle, and given a high polish. We were more than relaxed; we were close to being rag dolls.

Collapsed on two armchairs under the colonnade, our feet sharing an ottoman, we sipped iced tea and made a dinner of the leftovers from the party, which Maria Elena ferried to us on platters from the kitchen.

"Isn't this guacamole heavenly?" Olga said, scooping up the dip with a cracker. "I am passionate about avocado, and the Hoffmanns' recipe is perfection."

"I'm partial to these *molotes* myself," I said, taking one of the little cornmeal dumplings filled with shredded pork. "Who knew I would fall in love with Mexican food?"

"Did you try the quesadillas yet?"

"No. Which ones are they?"

"Those little triangles. They're like a Mexican version of a grilled cheese sandwich, only using tortillas and in this case, I think, chicken and peppers."

"I'm getting an education in Mexican cuisine just from your party," I said. "It was a wonderful party, in case I forgot to thank you."

"You didn't forget. You've already thanked me, and it's I who should thank you. I don't know what I would have done with myself alone today if you hadn't been here to keep me company."

"I imagine you would have done pretty much the same things that we did together."

"But it's more fun when you can share them," she said, trying unsuccessfully to stifle a yawn. "Oh, excuse me. I'm going to make up tonight for all the sleep I lost this week worrying about Vaughan."

"That sounds like an excellent idea," I said.

"We took care of me today," Olga said. "What would *you* like to do tomorrow? You name it, Jessica, and I'll arrange it. Anything—anything at all."

"It seems to me I got the benefit of all the things you wanted to do today," I said. "But since you're offering, let's see. I'd like to play tourist for a few hours, visit the landmarks, pick up a few gifts for people back home. But if that's not your cup of tea, I can always do it another day when you and Vaughan have plans."

"No such thing," she said. "I'll be delighted to play tourist with you as long as we can go shopping afterward. We'll consult the visitors' guides and plan out a morning of sightseeing. I'm not sure if there's a museum, but I know there are plenty of galleries if you like to 'appreciate' art. Then we'll have a nice *comida*. I know just the place."

"And *comida* is?"

"*Comida corrida* is a formal lunch, a midday meal with three or four set courses—soup, pasta, main course, dessert. They make the greatest flan. We won't want dinner after that, but we may need a little siesta—big meals always make me sleepy—but we can rest up in El Jardin. It's a stone's throw away."

"That lovely park near the police station."

"Yes. Then, if we haven't exhausted ourselves, we go shopping," she said, grinning. She pointed her toes and rotated her feet so she could study them from different angles. "I think I'd like to find a new pair of sandals, something a little sexier than what I've been wearing. Have to keep Vaughan on his toes. Can't let his eye wander. I think he's feeling his age."

"What makes you say that?" I said. "He's more handsome and energetic than men half his age."

"He is, isn't he?" Olga said, smiling coyly. "And he still attracts a lot of women. I'm thinking of one in particular. You may have noticed her interest."

"Sarah Christopher."

Olga saluted me. "I knew you'd see through her. A little obvious, isn't she?"

"I don't think you have a thing to worry about," I said.

"She's having a good time practicing her wiles on him."

"Unsuccessfully, I might add. Vaughan all but ran in the opposite direction when she flirted with him last night."

"She makes him uncomfortable—for now. Let's hope it stays that way."

"He knows how lucky he is to have you for his wife."

"And I want to keep it that way. I don't like being jealous, Jessica. I'm used to being indifferent to all the women who throw themselves at him. I trust Vaughan and I know he loves me. But somehow with Sarah it's different."

"Perhaps it's not only Vaughan who's feeling his age."

"You know, J. B. Fletcher, sometimes you're *too* observant," she said, arching an eyebrow at me. "Let me keep *some* of my secrets, please." She pulled a pillow from behind her back and hugged it to her chest. "You're right, of course. I don't envy who she is, mind you, but I'll admit to being jealous of her age." She sighed. "I never used to feel that way. I was always determined to gracefully accept whatever changes aging brought. I take care of myself, but I won't go to extremes to appear to be anything but what I am. Still, lately I've been wondering what I'd do if I had the chance to start all over again. Would I make the same decisions? Would I go off in another direction altogether? I dream about being young again."

"There's no harm in dreaming," I said. "Most of us have thoughts like that from time to time. The key is not to give them too much importance in your life today. After all, we can't change what was; we can only change what will be. Besides, it's never too late to take a new direction. Look at you and Vaughan. You've found a home in Mexico. You're learning a new language, making new friends, even discovering new artists whose work appeals to you."

Olga laughed, as I'd hoped she would. "She is talented, isn't she? Too bad she has a crush on my husband." She took a sip of her iced tea and set it down with a bang. "I'm going to spend Vaughan's money on pretty sandals tomorrow." Her eyes were full of mischief. "Something that will make him come panting after his wife. Will you help me pick them out?"

"I think I'd better leave that choice to you," I said. "But you can help me buy a new pair of earrings. I saw the perfect pair in a shop window we passed yesterday."

"It's a deal."

"This area of central Mexico was inhabited by nomadic Indians before a Franciscan missionary, Juan de San Miguel, founded a community here in the fifteen hundreds and called it San Miguel de Grande. He and his fellow friars converted the Indians to Christianity and taught them how to grow crops and weave fabrics. Ranches were established and tanneries built. The town became a commercial center, a successful market in which textiles and cattle were bought and sold. It was also a stopover for those seeking their fortunes from the silver deposits discovered in Zacatecas. But its real claim to fame is that it played an important role in Mexican independence."

Olga and I sat on a bench in El Jardin and eavesdropped on a tour guide as he gave his speech to a clutch of visitors he was leading through the park. Children were chasing each other around the gazebo or begging their mothers for balloons or treats from the sellers of cotton candy and ice cream. A woman sold roasted corn on the cob on a stick. A three-man mariachi band serenaded a couple in wedding dress having their photograph taken.

We had already spent the morning walking around San Miguel. We'd paused by the *lavandería*, watching women bent over cement tubs taking advantage of El Chorro, a natural spring that bubbles up, to do their wash and laugh and gossip with their friends. We'd strolled through the Parque Benito Juárez across the street, where flower growers from the countryside had set up an informal nursery, adding the brilliant colors of their bouquets and potted plants to the lush landscaping of the park. We'd admired the student paintings at Bellas Artes, a prestigious art school. We'd toured and shopped (Olga didn't want to chance tiring before that), had eaten a huge meal, and were happy to simply sit and digest while the parade of characters that daily crosses the stage that is El Jardín entertained us.

"A brave revolutionary general, Ignacio de Allende y Unzaga, a citizen of San Miguel, joined his army with the followers of Father Don Miguel Hidalgo of the town of Dolores to rise up against the Spanish ruling class. The patriots eventually gathered a force of eighty thousand. Sadly, it was not enough. They were defeated and the leaders were executed for their part in the revolt. It was many bloody years before independence was achieved, but the people never forgot their heroism. Today we call our town San Miguel de Allende in honor of the general."

The tourists trailed after their leader, who held aloft a red umbrella so those in the back could see where he was. He guided them across the street to La Parroquia. The name indicates it's a parish church, but it seemed more like a cathedral to me. It's the city's most famous landmark, and images of its fluted spires and turrets grace nearly every postcard sold in San Miguel. I had bought three views of it that morning to send as greetings to friends in Cabot Cove, although if all the complaints I'd heard at the party about the Mexican postal service were true, I would likely be back home long before the cards arrived.

"So you like my purchase?" Olga asked, peeking into her shopping bag where her new pastel platform sandals were nestled in tissue paper. Their long strands of soft cord were meant to lace up the calf and draw the eye from the foot to the ankle to the leg.

"Very elegant," I said, watching the groom select a colorful balloon for his bride. His sky blue tuxedo contrasted with the drab clothing worn by the vendor, whose back was to me. The groom said something to the man, who laughed, his shoulders bouncing up and down, causing the balloons to dance gaily on their strings.

"Are you sure you'll be able to walk in those shoes on the cobblestones?" I asked Olga.

"Not really," she said, her brow knitted. "I'll have to save them for an evening when I know we're taking a cab to a restaurant."

"Or wait to wear them in New York," I said.

The photographer beckoned to the bridal couple, who posed with their balloon. There was something about the vignette that kept my attention riveted.

"At that price, I'll make sure I wear them somewhere," Olga said, patting the tissue paper back in place. "I'm glad you found such pretty earrings, but I'm miffed you didn't let me buy them for you."

"You're very generous," I said, "but I can't think of a single reason why you should buy me earrings."

"I wanted to replace the ones that were stolen."

"You weren't responsible for that, Olga. But now that you've raised the topic, do you see those people?"

"The bride and groom? How sweet! He gave her a balloon."

"Do you recognize anyone there?"

"I've never seen them," she said.

"That balloon man," I said. "I think I've seen him before."

"He must have been here when you went to the police station the other day."

"No. I would have remembered that."

"Why does it matter?"

"If I'm not mistaken, he may be the man who robbed us."

"Omigod! Do you want me to get the police?" She started to rise, but I put my hand out to stop her.

"I can't be certain," I said. "It was night and I never saw the *bandido*'s face."

"Then what makes you think he's the one?"

I shrugged. "It's more a feeling than a positive identification," I said, hesitating. "But the hat is right, and he's wearing a plaid kerchief around his neck."

"That's pretty common around here, Jessica."

"So Chief Rivera said."

"Well, let's let the police question him; then you'll know."

I shook my head. "I can't go to the police on a hunch. It wouldn't be fair to the man."

The vendor glanced over his shoulder, perhaps conscious that he was being observed. His eyes met mine briefly and he turned away.

Olga shivered. "He has such cold eyes. What should we do, Jessica?"

"I'm afraid there's nothing we can do," I said, patting her arm. "Chief Rivera said there was no hope for recovering my belongings, and even less for bringing the thief to justice."

"Has the incident spoiled the trip for you?"

"Of course not, Olga. It was a momentary distraction. I'm sorry if I upset you."

"Well, aren't we a pair," she said, relaxing back on the bench. "I worry about you and you worry about me. I think it's time we moseyed on home."

"Yes. You don't want to miss Vaughan's call," I said.

"That, and I want to look through the copy of *The World's Best Bartenders' Guide* we bought today. I'm going to experiment tonight and make us margaritas."

"That's getting into the spirit of Mexico," I said.

Olga laughed and picked up her shopping bag. "Literally and figuratively."

I glanced back to see where the balloon vendor was, but he'd left the park.

"I wonder . . ." I said to myself as I followed Olga down the path.

At the corner I spotted him again. He was across the

street waiting for a bus to pass by. His back was to me, but I could see his shoulders moving up and down, his balloons bouncing merrily in the warm afternoon air as they'd done when he'd talked with the groom. It was only then that it struck me. The balloon man hadn't been laughing. He'd been coughing.

Chapter Ten

"We're leaving first thing in the morning," Vaughan had told Olga. "By the dawn's early light, if I can get Woody moving that fast. We should be home tomorrow night by seven, eight at the latest. I'll call you if there's any change in plans."

Olga had been singing all day. She'd tried on her new sandals and modeled them for Maria Elena and me, strutting across the courtyard and striking a pose under the colonnade, just as she had in her runway days when she was a high-fashion model.

"She is still so beautiful, yes?" Maria Elena said to me.

"Inside and out," I agreed.

"She has been very kind to me and my family. And Mr. Buckley, of course, he has been most kind. My brother Hector, I think he has a secret love for her. But many men do. I see how they gaze at her when she is not looking. In New York, it is the same, yes?"

"I would imagine it is," I said, "but I don't live in New York anymore, so I don't get to see them as often as I used to."

Olga stepped out of her new sandals and came into the kitchen. "Ladies, you are going to have to excuse me. I have a date at the hair salon. José is fitting me in, and I don't want to keep him waiting."

Once Olga was gone, Maria Elena showed me how to access my e-mail, and I spent the afternoon in Vaughan's media room answering correspondence, checking in with my agent, and dropping a note to my dear friend and Cabot Cove's favorite physician, Seth Hazlitt. I gave him a brief rundown of my activities in San Miguel and sent the Buckleys' regards, which I knew they'd want me to do. I omitted the incident with the *bandido*. I didn't want to upset him. There would be time enough when I got home to recount the lurid details. He would sputter, but he'd also see that I was none the worse for the experience.

I have learned over the years that I can live through the unpleasant, put it behind me, and move on. Others may dwell on ugly events, may let them color the rest of their lives, but I will not. Life is too precious to waste on worry and regrets. The death of my husband, Frank, taught me that lesson many years ago, and I've taken it to heart.

When Olga returned, coiffed and elegantly made up, she opted to wait dinner for Vaughan. She had Maria Elena set the table under the colonnade instead of in the dining room, where they usually took their evening meals. I declined her invitation to join them and ate early, planning to retire to the guest room with a book I'd brought with me. I wanted to give my hosts the opportunity for a private reunion.

"It's really not necessary," Olga said. "Vaughan and I always enjoy your company."

"That's very kind of you to say," I replied, "but I carried this hardback with me all the way from New York and promised myself I wouldn't leave San Miguel until I'd finished reading it. At the rate I'm going, you may have to keep me as a guest for a month or more."

"That wouldn't be a sacrifice."

"You enjoy your dinner with Vaughan. He can tell me all about Woody and their exploits over breakfast."

The guest room had been decorated with a visitor's comfort in mind, down to a chaise longue in the corner and a bath en suite, as they say in hotel brochures. I took advantage of the latter, soaking in scented bubbles and choosing a loofah from the array of bath items Olga had considerately placed in a basket by the tub for her guests. Scrubbed, perfumed, and in my nightclothes, I settled down on the chaise to discover that Maria Elena had left a cup of tea and a plate of crescent cookies next to my book while I was in the bath.

At seven, I heard the telephone ring and the patter of Olga's sandals on the floor as she ran to answer it.

At eight, Maria Elena knocked at my door and asked if I wanted more tea.

I looked up from my book. "No, thank you. I'm fine," I said. "The cookies were delicious."

She started to say something, changed her mind, and closed the door softly.

At nine, Olga went into the media room and selected an album of orchestral pieces by Debussy. The music flowed through the house, and although there wasn't a speaker in my room, I could hear the strains of the composition through the door. I smiled, picturing the Buckleys clinking wineglasses and toasting Vaughan's safe return.

An hour and a half later, the music was shut off and the rumble of thunder took its place. I set my book aside, went into the bathroom, cleaned my teeth, ran a brush through my hair, and flipped the light switch off. My mind was filled with the chapters I'd just read, and I was surprised to hear another knock on my door.

"Come in."

"Jessica, may I talk to you?"

"Certainly, Olga. Is something wrong?"

"Vaughan isn't home yet. He hasn't called and I'm worried."

"I thought I heard the phone earlier."

"It wasn't Vaughan. Someone from *Noticias* called and started asking for Vaughan. I cut him off, said to try back tomorrow. I didn't want Vaughan to phone and find the line busy. What's the point of a subscription anyway, when we're here so rarely?"

"It's a funny time to call for a subscription," I said.

"At home those sales calls interrupt our dinner two or three times a week."

"I'm just surprised to hear it's the same in San Miguel."

Olga shrugged. "Vaughan said he'd call if there was any change in their itinerary. I haven't heard from him and it's starting to rain."

"If there's bad weather in the mountains, that alone may have slowed them down. I'm sure there's nothing wrong. Cellular service isn't perfect. My phone didn't work when Juanito and I were stranded." I regretted my words immediately.

She looked confused. "Who? Oh, yes, the young man who drove you from León. Heavens! Don't remind me. You don't think they were attacked by *bandidos,* do you?"

"My guess would be they got a late start and forgot to call. Or perhaps they tried and couldn't get through."

"The phones are not as reliable as in the States."

"There you are. They're probably frustrated at not being able to contact you."

"You think so?"

"I do."

"I'm sorry to have disturbed you."

"Don't give it another thought."

She shifted from one foot to the other. "Are you enjoying your book?"

"Very much, but I've read enough for tonight. Would you like me to wait with you till Vaughan arrives?"

"Would you? He makes me so mad. He knows I'm a worrier. They should have pulled off the road into a gas station, or somewhere else with a telephone on a land line. I know I'm being a wimp, but I won't feel right till he walks through the door."

"I understand. We can watch a movie if you like. It might help to pass the time. There's quite a collection in the media room. I was looking at all your videos this afternoon."

"I don't think I can sit still for TV. Do you mind?"

"Of course not. I'll get dressed and meet you downstairs." I pulled on the first thing that came to hand, my jogging suit, slipped a cardigan over my shoulders, and closed the door behind me.

I found Olga pacing barefoot in the kitchen, her new sandals discarded in the corner. "Did you have anything to eat yet?" I asked.

"I can't eat till Vaughan gets home," she said. "Besides, it's probably all dried out by now. Maria Elena put dinner in the oven to keep it warm, but that was hours ago. I told her not to wait up. Who knows what time he'll arrive?"

"Have you called the police?"

"Do you think I should?"

"You did when I was late," I said, not bothering to point out that it was almost morning when we were found. "Woody's station wagon is not exactly the latest model. If they've broken down on the road and their phones don't work, they'll be grateful for help."

Her face brightened. "I hadn't thought of that. I was picturing the worst-case scenario. That old clunker—isn't that what Sarah calls it?—it's a breakdown waiting to happen. Just because the outside doesn't have holes in it doesn't mean the engine's without rot. That must be it."

She dialed the operator and asked to be connected to the *delegación,* using her newly learned Spanish. She covered the mouthpiece with her hand and said to me, "I hope someone there speaks English. My Spanish isn't very good. I don't even know how to say 'traffic accident.' " She turned her attention to the voice on the other end of the line. "*Sí. Mi nombre es Olga Buckley. Mi marido pierde,*" she said slowly, rolling her R's. "Oh, dear, he's speaking too fast. *No entiendo.* I don't understand. *¿Habla inglés? Soy Americana.*"

There was a long pause while the dispatcher went to find someone who spoke English.

"I don't want to disturb Maria Elena," she said to me, "but I may have to if they can't find someone I can talk to. You know, I really didn't think about this when Vaughan and I decided to buy the house. We assumed we'd take classes, learn Spanish at our leisure, and practice on everyone around us. I don't know why I didn't think about what would happen if there was an emergency. I can't believe we were so foolish."

"It seems to me that Maria Elena is the perfect person to help in an emergency, and you were very sensible to hire her. But I'm not sure we can call Vaughan being late an emergency. Not yet, anyway."

Olga nodded, gave me a brief smile, and listened intently to the voice on the telephone. The police had provided someone who spoke a little English. Olga spoke a little Spanish. In fits and starts, and in both languages, they carried on a conversation. She didn't know Woody's license plate number but was able to provide a good description of the car, of her husband, and of Woody, and a brief explanation of why they were on the road at night. "*Ellos*—oh, what's the word for 'driving'?—*manejan*—that's right—*manejan de Laredo*, uh, *de Monterrey*."

The policeman promised to send someone out to look, and they rang off.

"Do you think he really will? Send someone out?" she fretted.

"We have to wait either way. I'm going to put on some water for tea. Would you like a cup?"

She nodded. "Use water from the pitcher in the fridge. We don't drink anything from the tap."

I brewed two cups of tea and we carried them into the living room. A large glass table sat between matching modern sofas covered in a narrow copper and teal stripe. Floral pillows in several shades of purple were tucked at either end. A pair of wooden armchairs with ocher cushions flanked the fireplace. Behind one was an elaborately carved chest placed against the wall. On its top, a colorful ceramic jug—probably the creation of another local artist—rested on a fabric square, embroidered in red in a design that also incorporated tiny mirrors. The mirrors reflected all the hues in the jug, making the fabric appear to be multicolored itself. A sisal rug covered part of the Saltillo-tiled floor. The room was elegant but spare. By far the biggest impact came from three large canvases that formed a triptych on the far wall, a historical panorama of San Miguel from the mountains down to the city. From the left to the right, they depicted rural life under the cruel Spanish overseers, then a revolutionary battle, the faces of the combatants contorted with the strain of wielding heavy weapons against their oppressors, and finally the city that grew up after the peace. Together they made a powerful statement, yet each could have stood alone as a complete painting.

"Those are by Sarah Christopher, I gather." They were much more somber and dramatic than the canvases on display in the dining room, but the style was unmistakable.

"You can see what a talent she is," Olga said. "We're missing her gallery opening tonight."

"She said she isn't satisfied with them and wanted to give our money back and take them away. But we love them. And we've already had two offers to buy them at double what we paid for them."

"Her work is a good investment."

"It is, but that's not why we support her. Vaughan teases me that I always wanted to be a patron of the arts, but in a sense we really are. She was struggling in the beginning, not in terms of money so much—her father still helps when she's tapped out—but in terms of recognition."

"Which will translate into money eventually," I said, "if it hasn't already."

"It has. When we discovered her, we bought these three early works and the more recent ones you saw in the dining room and hall, and then we threw a big housewarming party for ourselves. We invited a crowd of people from the expat community as well as her instructors at Bellas Artes and people we'd met at Instituto Allende in our Spanish class. There must have been as many people as we had for you the other day, but they were all inside because it was pouring. I couldn't have planned it better myself."

"So she got a lot of business from your guests."

"It's what we wanted to happen, not to boost our investment but because we wanted to see her succeed. She's not a dilettante. She's a genuine artist. She works from morning till night and usually has at least two paintings in progress."

"I imagine being young and a woman makes it more difficult to break into established art circles," I said.

"Not so much here in San Miguel," she said, "but you're right when it comes to the outside world—New York, for instance. We sponsored her first showing at a gallery on Madison Avenue where we know the owner. The critics who came—and only a few did—were lukewarm about her talent. They were looking for something more avant-garde. Paintings like hers, rendered with sensitivity and insight, not to mention having recognizable figures in them, didn't suit their expectations."

"That must happen fairly frequently," I said. "There are so many talented artists, and so few are able to break out and make a name for themselves beyond their own community."

"I still think she has a chance to do that, but now it's going to take more politics than talent. She has to pursue it. And it takes time away from the art. That's where most artists fall down—in promoting themselves. We can't be her agents, although we were happy to sponsor her initial show."

"I would think she'd be very grateful to you," I said, remembering that Sarah's behavior at the party didn't strike me as appreciative in any way that would be appropriate.

As if reading my mind, Olga said, "She's very self-centered, as many artists are, if I can get away with generalizing like that."

Olga's nerves were not on display as we sipped our tea and talked about art and San Miguel. I didn't know if she was putting on an act for my benefit or if she had determined not to make herself crazy with fretting. I was aware, however, that the evening was lengthening and we hadn't heard from either Vaughan or Woody, much less the San Miguel police. *If the car broke down early in their trip from Monterrey,* I reasoned, *they may be contending with unfamiliar territory, as well as local authorities with little concern for their travel schedule. However,* I argued with myself, *the Mexican people I've met were willing to go out of their way to help a stranger. Surely someone would have volunteered to make a telephone call to assist stranded visitors.*

With no clear idea of what had happened and a mounting sense of unease, I felt the best thing I could do to help was to keep Olga occupied until we heard something, or until my voice gave out. I guided the conversation around to people we both knew in New York and whom I had seen on my last book tour.

"Your videotape from the *Today* show," she moaned. "We completely forgot to watch it, Jessica."

"There's no hurry," I said.

"But you brought it all the way from New York."

"Only because it was easier to pack it than find a way to send it home. I'll leave it with you. You can mail it back whenever you like, or even wait till we see each other again. My agent's secretary always gets video clips of my media appearances. Last year she sent them all to me on a single DVD."

"Technology seems to evolve so quickly these days, doesn't it?" Olga said. "We've got a lot of movies on videotape, but now they're all being issued on DVD. Which reminds me—I found the perfect place for those gorgeous bookends you brought. Did you see them?"

"In the media room."

"But they're holding up *books*," she said, smiling.

A tap at the front door interrupted us. Olga bolted from her seat and raced to answer it. Apparently her calm façade had been a ruse.

"Mrs. Buckley?"

I recognized the voice of Chief Rivera and hurried to join her.

"Mrs. Fletcher. Nice to see you again," he said, saluting me with his index finger. Javier Rivera wore a polo shirt and blue jeans. A damp raincoat was draped over one arm. *He must have been called away from home,* I thought. Behind him were two young officers in blue slacks and white shirts that stuck to their skin where the rain had made large wet patches.

"May I come in?"

Olga pulled the door wide, her face suddenly pale.

The chief came inside but left his escorts in the courtyard.

"Did you find them?" I said, giving voice to what Olga was afraid to ask.

"Let me ask the questions, please. Can we find a place to sit down?"

Olga led us into the kitchen. Its homey warmth was usually comforting, but tonight a sour tang from leftover food hung in the air and made the room feel cold and un-welcoming. She picked up the sandals she'd left on the floor and ran a hand over the table as if to wipe away a nonexist-ent spill.

Rivera held a chair for her and cocked his head toward me. I pulled my chair next to hers and she reached over to grip my hand.

"Mrs. Buckley, can you tell me where your husband went and why, when he was expected back, and why you called the authorities?"

Olga cleared her throat and gave Rivera a summary of the reasons for the mail run; she told him that her husband and Woody Manheim, who was driving his own car, were supposed to have left Monterrey at dawn and should have been back by seven, that they hadn't called, and that she was sorry if she shouldn't have called the police. But she was worried when it got late, she said, so she called and asked the police to check the road in case the car had broken down and they needed help.

Rivera stood nearby and listened carefully, nodding his head to indicate that he understood and to encourage her to continue.

"Did you find them?" she asked, jumping up and put-ting a hand on his arm, her eyes pleading. "Are they all right?"

His gaze met hers, and she backed away. "Yes and no," he said softly.

"What does that mean?" I asked, getting up to stand next to Olga.

"It means we haven't found them yet."

"But you found something, didn't you, Chief Rivera?" I said.

He didn't answer. Instead he said to Olga, "I think you'd better sit down, Mrs. Buckley."

"I don't want to sit down. Tell me what it is. Tell me what you found."

Rivera reached into his pocket and pulled out a plastic bag. "Do you recognize this?" he asked gently.

"Omigod," Olga whispered, her knees giving way.

Inside the clear plastic was a cotton handkerchief with crocheted edging and an embroidered O in the corner. It was the handkerchief Olga had pressed into Vaughan's hand the morning he'd left, the one she'd given him as a remembrance of her. It had once been white, but now it was hard to tell what the original color had been. It was stained a dark crimson by blood—a lot of blood.

Chapter Eleven

"We found the car and the handkerchief. There was no sign of either man."

"Does that mean they're alive?" Olga asked.

"I can't promise you that," Rivera said. His eyes were sympathetic.

"Is it a kidnapping?" I asked.

"That's what I'm thinking." He turned to Olga. "But there's no way to confirm it unless they contact you, Mrs. Buckley."

Maria Elena took the blanket from her own shoulders and wrapped it around Olga, rubbing her hands up and down Olga's arms. She'd been roused from her sleep by the sound of voices in her kitchen and a flashing red light from the police car in the street sweeping over the walls of her room. She'd entered just as the police chief pulled the bloody handkerchief from his pocket. She was visibly upset, but she focused on the needs of her employer, wiping away her own tears while trying to comfort Olga.

"Will they deliver a ransom note?" Olga asked.

"More likely a telephone call. They're not going to want to be seen near the house. Sometimes they even e-mail these days. I would've expected to find something in the car. My guys gave it a thorough going-over, but there wasn't any message, nothing at all, other than a bunch of boxes of magazines and catalogs and a few stray pieces of mail."

"Wasn't there more mail than that?" I asked.

"No. They probably took it to rummage through for checks or cash."

"Where did you find the handkerchief?" I asked.

"Under the front of the car. Someone may have deliberately placed it there to keep the rain from washing away the blood. It looks to me as though they wanted it found to make their point."

Olga shivered.

"What are you going to do now?" I asked the police chief.

"We can't do anything tonight. It's pitch-black out there, and the rain has already washed away any evidence we might have found at the scene—footprints, stains, things like that. I've posted two men to stay with the car to make sure *it* doesn't disappear. I'm surprised they didn't take it along with its occupants."

"What's the next step?" I asked.

"I'll go back out first thing in the morning to see if there's anything we might have missed."

"I'd like to go with you," I said.

"I don't see the point, but if it will make you feel better, all right."

I thought back to my introduction to him. He'd indicated he wouldn't mind enjoying the sort of challenges the police in Mexico City regularly confront. But the events of this evening made changing jurisdictions unnecessary to satisfy his thirst for action. He was faced with the likely kidnapping of two American men—and, I had to silently add, the possibility of murder—which was undoubtedly more challenging than logging the lost belongings of a tourist from the States who'd been the quarry of a highway bandit.

But his expression said that he wasn't enjoying this. The thrill of working on a serious case had a dark side—the necessity of dealing with victims or, in this case, the family of victims. It meant delivering bad news and watching people suffer. Chief Rivera obviously took no pleasure in such tasks. But he was a professional, and I was certain he would do what was required of him. He knew the ins and outs of law enforcement, spoke the language, and had been in Mexico long enough to have developed contacts. I hoped that he could put those attributes to good use and would find Vaughan and Woody—alive.

"I should go with you, shouldn't I?" Olga asked. "Vaughan might have left me a clue that no one else would recognize. It would be just like him to do something like that."

He already did, I thought, thinking of the handkerchief.

"It's more important for you to stay home, Olga," I said. "You're needed here in case anyone tries to contact you."

"You're right, of course," she said. "I'll stay here. Vaughan may be lost and trying to find his way back." To Maria Elena she said, "Would you get me a sweater, please? It's suddenly gotten very cold."

I took her hands in mine. They were like ice, and she shivered despite the heavy blanket enfolding her. I realized she was in shock.

"Do you have any brandy?" I asked Maria Elena. "And something for her to eat?"

"I don't want anything," Olga said. "I want my mind clear in case I can help Vaughan."

"You can help Vaughan by taking care of yourself and not getting sick," I said. "You need to eat, and to rest."

"I'll be going now," Rivera said, shrugging into his raincoat. He left a card on the table next to Olga's chair. "A patrol car will pass by the house every half hour, just to keep an eye out. That's my cell phone number. Call me if you hear from your husband or anyone else regarding this. If anything strikes you as being unusual or suspicious, call immediately. Don't open the door for tradesmen or anyone else you don't know personally."

"All right," she said. She looked up at Maria Elena. "Maybe a little brandy would be good."

She looked exhausted. There were dark circles under her eyes, and her hair hung lank; the elegant coiffure the hairdresser had carefully created was now a casualty of Olga's nervous hands. My heart ached for her.

"I'm going to walk the chief out," I said. "I'll be back in a few minutes."

"What am I going to do without Vaughan?" she said absently, more to herself than to us.

"Don't give up on him," I said. "We'll find him." I prayed I was right and that we wouldn't be too late.

At the door I asked the police chief what I couldn't say in front of Olga. "I know this is an unfair question, Chief, but please be candid with me. From what you know about this type of crime in Mexico, how often is a kidnap victim found alive?"

He ran his hand over the rough stubble of whiskers on his chin. "It depends. If you mean found alive without handing over any money? Rarely. If you mean released after a ransom is paid? I gotta be honest with you. That doesn't always happen. But I'll tell you this, Mrs. Fletcher. We'll give it everything we've got. I'll call in the AFI. That's the Mexican FBI. I'll drill my guys to work their snitches. We'll comb the streets and turn over all the rocks." He opened the door and pulled up the collar of his coat. "Really coming down now," he said, peering into the veil of water sweeping over the courtyard stones. "Good thing we found the handkerchief before it got washed away."

"There's another good thing," I said.

"What's that?"

"That they were taken near San Miguel. That means someone here might know something."

He grunted. "If they'd disappeared out of my jurisdiction, I wouldn't be much help to you. But if they're in my backyard, we'll find them. One way or another, we'll find them."

"What time should I be ready for you in the morning?"

He glanced at his watch. "You're sure you want to do this? You're not going to get much sleep tonight."

"I wouldn't anyway."

"Good morning," I said four hours later as I climbed into the backseat of Chief Rivera's cruiser.

The morning air was sharp and clear, carrying the sound of church bells tolling all over the city. I knew they were a daily, in some cases hourly, occurrence, but the deep reverberations made me shiver. I hoped they weren't an omen of things to come.

After the chief had left I sat with Olga for a long time. There was little more to say until circumstances became clearer, but I'd told her we were lucky to have Rivera working for us and that I would do everything in my power to help him find Vaughan and Woody.

Maria Elena had given Olga a snifter of brandy and coaxed her to eat some toast. She'd stayed with her through the night, dozing in a chair by the bed where Olga, curled in a ball, slept fitfully, waking with a start every few minutes at some sound, real or imagined.

Rivera drove. His second in command, Captain Gutierrez, whom I'd met at the police station, yawned loudly from the passenger seat and scratched his chest. He rattled off something in Spanish, causing Rivera to frown.

The car bounced over the cobblestones, making conversation difficult. Rivera gunned the engine and took the corners at what I considered an unsafe speed in light of the uneven road. If there were any springs left in the suspension of the cruiser, they didn't have much "spring" anymore. Every jolt and thud threw me up to the roof and down again. I hung on to a strap above the window and tried not to fall off the bench seat, praying my breakfast wouldn't make another appearance.

Away from the center of town the road smoothed out and I released my hold on the strap.

"You okay back there?" Rivera called over his shoulder.

"I am now. That was quite a bumpy ride."

"There was a movement a while back to pave over those cobblestones," he said. "All the ladies who want to wear high heels joined in, claimed the streets were unsafe for walking. They have to take cabs wherever they go downtown."

I leaned forward. "What happened?"

He laughed. "The tourists objected. They didn't want the city to remove any of the 'charm.' The preservationists had a fit, but you'd expect that. In the end, it was the taxi drivers who made sure the measure never got anywhere. Those cobblestones guarantee lots of business for them."

"And for the owners of car repair shops, I imagine."

"By the way, I learned a little something about you, Mrs. Fletcher, that you neglected to tell me earlier."

"What's that?"

"You're a famous author. You forgot to mention that when you filed the report. You just said you were a professor at Manhattan University."

"Actually, Chief, I *did* teach at the university when I lived in Manhattan. That's true."

"Yeah, but what you didn't say is what you usually do for a living."

"You didn't ask."

The high desert had swallowed up the rain from the night before. There was no trace of the torrents that had cascaded down the hills and across the road, except for a dusty residue that had already been kicked up by early-morning trucks bringing goods to town. At the site where Woody's car had been abandoned, the ground was as dry as if the rain had fallen a week earlier rather than the night before.

Two men in khaki uniforms squatted by a small campfire they'd built a short distance from their official car. They stood and stretched when we pulled in.

"*Transito* police," Rivera said by way of explanation. "They found the car. They're not under my command, but I asked them to keep watch till I could relieve them this morning."

The men exchanged greetings with Rivera and Gutierrez, kicked sand on the embers of their campfire, and left in their vehicle.

"Do you know this car at all?" Rivera asked, cocking his head toward Woody's station wagon.

"The only time I saw it was when they left on their trip," I said. "Three days ago."

"Anything look different?"

I walked around the car and thought back to the morning Vaughan and Woody had started out, Vaughan eager for adventure and Woody proud to provide it. The rain had washed off the top layer of dust, but the faded blue paint was no brighter. I peered through the windows and saw the jumble of cartons that had been used to sort the mail of families with post office boxes in Laredo.

"Their luggage is gone," I said.

"What did it look like?" Rivera asked, motioning to Gutierrez, who pulled a pad and pen out of his pocket.

Gutierrez had ignored me during the drive. I wasn't sure if he was resentful of my presence or was simply an unpleasant person. I had tried to enlist his opinion on the incident, but he'd either refused to respond or glared at Rivera when the chief answered my questions. Now he listened.

"Woody's bag was a military duffel, medium size, olive drab with nylon straps for handles and a metal zipper across the top," I said. "It was pretty old, worn around the edges." I waited while his writing caught up to my description. "Vaughan's bag was a satchel, tweed with tan leather trim. The brand is Hartmann, I think."

"Figures," Rivera said. "That told them right away that the guy's got dough."

Rivera said something to Gutierrez in Spanish, causing the officer to pocket his pad and open the car's front door.

"I told him to check the glove box and the floor of the car before the lab guys go over it," Rivera said to me. "We've got to wait for the tow truck. Want to take a walk?"

The car had been forced off the road where the land was flat. About thirty feet from the roadbed there was a gentle slope, the land littered with scrub trees and brush, an easy place for kidnappers to hide while waiting for the arrival of their victims. The morning was quiet, except for the rustle of dried branches as they rubbed against each other in the breeze. The sky was a vivid blue, broken only by the dark silhouette of a bird of prey circling overhead

"When my driver and I were stopped by the bandit," I said, "he'd placed a boulder in the middle of the road to force us to swerve to avoid hitting it. Do you think the kidnappers might have done the same thing?"

"Could be, but it would be easier just to put out a flare or something to indicate there was a problem ahead. Sometimes they have someone lie down in the middle of the road pretending to be injured, pour ketchup or salsa on him to look like blood. They leave a car on the side, like there's just been an accident. Anyone coming on that would slow down. It's human nature. That's all they need to pounce."

I paused next to a bush where several small branches had been snapped off recently. Cows wandered freely here. Did an animal do this?

"How many people might be involved?" I asked, extricating a few curly white hairs caught on the end of a broken twig.

"More than a couple, that's for sure," he said, walking ahead and turning to wait for me. "They never rely on even odds. It would be taking a chance with two men in the car. They'd want backup, want to surround them to keep them from escaping. I'd figure there were four, possibly five."

"Maybe Vaughan and Woody tried to escape," I said,

catching up and handing him the white strands. "These didn't come from a cow."

"I'd say you're right," he said, pulling an empty plastic bag from his jacket pocket and depositing my discovery inside.

"The car had fake sheepskin covers on the front seats," I said. "Do you think they might be from that?"

"Could be," he said. He cupped his eyes and scanned the countryside. "If they tried to get away," he said, "the only way they could run would be down this hill."

We started walking again, down the hill, taking a route that wouldn't even qualify as a trail. The terrain was rough, rocky, and unforgiving. We paused and looked back to where Gutierrez stood next to the car giving instructions to a tow truck operator. He glanced our way and shook his head.

"Do you think someone followed them from the hotel?" I asked, leaning against a boulder to shake a pebble from my shoe. "How else would they know about the luggage?"

The sun was getting higher now. I squinted against the glare. A second bird had joined the first and they floated over a stand of bushes in our path, their broad wings tipping from side to side in the air currents that rose from the hot earth. I walked ahead of Rivera.

"This type of crime is not spur of the moment," he said, following me. "These guys plan it out, know where to make their move, do it at night when they won't be seen or followed. They have to know their victim is worth the effort.

And they may not even contact the family. They might just swim their fish to an ATM machine and hold a gun to his head, shoot off his fingers one by one till he empties his bank account. Buckley's a prize. I don't know how much they can wring out of Manheim."

The birds were circling lower and I could see the red heads now and the wing tips spread like the fingers of a hand, the distinguishing marks of a particular kind of bird, a carrion eater, a vulture. Then I saw the object of their fascination. I gasped. My stomach dropped and my pulse quickened.

Rivera came up behind me. "They won't be getting any money from that one," he said.

Sadly I turned away from the body.

Chapter Twelve

The house was bustling with visitors when I returned: Dina and Roberto Fisher, Sarah Christopher, Cathie Harrison and Eric Gewirtz, Guy and Nancy Kovach, one couple whom I hadn't met but had seen at the party, and several others whose faces were new to me. They were gathered in the living room, chairs from the kitchen carried in to supplement the seating.

I left Chief Rivera in the vestibule and went in search of Olga. Maria Elena met me in the hall, balancing a tray of drinks and a bowl of cookies

"Word travels fast, doesn't it?" I said to her.

Her eyes flew to the ceiling and she blew a puff of air into her bangs, ruffling the wisps of hair on her forehead.

"Where is Mrs. Buckley?" I asked.

"Upstairs. She is packing."

"Packing? Why?"

"She goes to get the money."

"Hello, Jessica," Sarah said, coming into the hall where Maria Elena and I were talking. She lifted the tray from Maria Elena's arms. "I'll take that in," she said. "After all, we're here to help."

"Have you heard from the kidnappers?" I asked Maria Elena in a low voice after Sarah had returned to the living room.

The housekeeper shook her head.

"How did all these people find out?"

"From the papers."

"The newspaper?"

She nodded.

The phone rang and Maria Elena went off to answer it.

"I think I'd better go find Olga," I said aloud to no one.

She was talking on the phone when I knocked, a valise open on her bed and a pile of clothes beside it. She motioned me into her room, pointed at a chair, and waved her hand in a circle as if to speed up the caller.

"Carter, don't argue with me," she told the man on the other end of the line, who I assumed was Vaughan's attorney, Carter Baker. "Just make sure the stock sale goes through and the money is put in our account. I'll sign the papers tomorrow." She paused. "No. I'm flying out of León in about three hours. Have a car waiting for me at the airport. That you can do."

A copy of *Noticias* had been left on her dresser. I picked up the English-language newspaper and scanned the lead story under the headline TWO KIDNAPPED OUTSIDE CITY. Beneath it: PERPETRATORS DEMAND A MILLION DOLLARS. The article said that New York publisher Vaughan Buckley, a part-time resident of SMA, had been taken prisoner, along with Woodrow Manheim, a permanent resident in the expatriate community, as the pair were returning from a short business trip to Laredo. A note the editors believed to be genuine had been dropped off at the newspaper office the previous evening, demanding a million dollars in U.S. currency and the release of revolutionary detainees being held in the Guanajuato jail. The note had threatened that if these conditions were not met, the men would be executed. It was signed "The Revolutionary Guanajuato Brigade."

"Carter, you can lecture me to your heart's content when I get in," Olga said, pulling her hand through her hair in exasperation. "You're holding me up right now. Okay, I promise. I'll call as soon as we touch down."

Olga had no sooner hung up than the phone rang again.

"I'll let Maria Elena get it," she said.

Dina walked in carrying a small package.

"Olga, we need to talk," I said.

"I don't have time to talk, Jessica. I'm due to leave here in fifteen minutes and I haven't finished packing."

"Here," Dina said, handing her the package. "It's the smallest English-Spanish dictionary I could find. It'll fit right in your purse."

"Thank you, Dina."

"You know that Nancy Kovach is downstairs with Guy. It's the first time I've ever seen her without all her diamonds."

Olga walked to her dresser and pulled open a drawer. "Well, this isn't exactly a party."

"I know," Dina said, biting her lip. "I had Roberto write out some phrases you may need, you know, when you're talking to the kidnappers. I put the paper inside the back cover."

"Thank you very much. Please tell him I'm almost ready."

Dina lingered by the door.

Sarah knocked on the doorframe. "Olga, a reporter from the Associated Press is on the line."

"I don't have time to talk. Would you deal with him, please?"

"Sure."

"Olga, what's going on?" I asked.

"We're driving her to the airport," Dina said.

Olga folded two lightweight sweaters and tucked them in her bag. "I've already called my stockbroker, and I just spoke with our lawyer. We're meeting with representatives from Interpol and from the State Department tomorrow morning. I have to make sure we have enough funds in our account when the kidnappers make their demands. I can only do that in New York."

I dropped the newspaper on the bed. "How do you know the people in this article are the kidnappers?"

"Look!" she said, pointing to the paper. "They knew about the ransom before I did."

"And have *you* heard from the kidnappers?"

She shook her head.

"Have you been in touch with Woody's son?" I asked. "Perhaps they contacted him."

She gasped. "No! I never called him." Stung by her own insensitivity, she reached for the phone. "I'll do that now."

"He wasn't home when we stopped by earlier on our way here," Dina said.

I didn't want to talk in front of Dina, but clearly she didn't want to leave. "This whole thing is just not right," I said. "You can't know if these people in the newspaper are who they say they are or if they're just taking advantage of the situation. They could be con men hoping to extort money out of you."

"Don't you think she should get the money anyway?" Dina asked. "Just in case?"

"I'm not going to tell you what to do," I said to Olga, "but if I were you, I wouldn't make any decisions until I had an opportunity to talk with the police downstairs. They may be aware of details that could put the situation in a different light."

"What details?" Dina said.

Maria Elena entered the room and held out a bottle of pills to Olga.

"You found them!" Olga cried. "Where were they?"

"In the downstairs bathroom," Maria Elena said. "You left them there the last time you were here."

Olga gave her a quick hug. "Thank you. You are just wonderful," she said. "I'll be finished in five minutes."

"Olga," I said, "we need to talk."

"I know, I know."

"Now."

"Now?"

"In private."

She studied my face for a second. "Of course," she said. "Ladies, will you please excuse us?" She held the door for Maria Elena and Dina and shut it behind them. "But you'll have to talk while I pack, Jessica, and you'll have to talk fast."

I took her hands and led her to the bed. "Please, sit down."

"Jessica, you're scaring me."

"Olga, we found Woody."

Her face lit up for a second until she realized I wasn't smiling. Then her hand covered her mouth. "Is he . . . ?"

I nodded. "Dead. We found his body a little way from the car. He was shot. It looked as if he might have been trying to get away."

"You didn't find Vaughan?"

"No."

"Thank God!"

"We looked for him," I said. "We scouted the surrounding area for about a quarter mile, but there were only three of us. Chief Rivera radioed for a larger search party and also called for a helicopter, but it will take some time. The helicopter has to come from León. He also said he'd see if there was a tracking dog available."

"Do you think there's a chance Vaughan got away?"

"We didn't see anything that might indicate that. Rivera feels that Vaughan is in the kidnappers' hands."

"Should I cancel my trip to New York?"

"Only you can make that decision," I said. "I just wanted you to know all the facts in advance."

She bowed her head and was silent for a moment. Then she sighed and looked up at me. "I can't sit around and wait, Jessica. It's been driving me crazy all morning. At least in New York I'll be taking action, doing something to help Vaughan. I'll be ready when the instructions come, no matter who delivers them. I don't care what it's going to cost. I want my husband back."

"I understand."

"I know it's asking a lot," she said, "but will you stay here in my place? You know best how to deal with the police. I don't. But I'm the only one who can handle our financial affairs back home."

"Of course I'll stay."

"And you'll call me as soon as you hear from the kidnappers?"

"You have my word."

"They'll be speaking Spanish, I'm sure, so you'll need Maria Elena to translate."

"We'll be fine."

She stood slowly, straightened her shoulders, and went to finish packing.

I opened the door to find Dina right outside.

"I was just about to knock," she said. "Roberto says he's ready whenever you are, Olga."

"Tell him I'll be down in a minute. I'm closing my bag now."

"You know, Jessica, Roberto is fluent in Spanish."

"I'll keep that in mind."

I watched Dina walk away. It was obvious to me that she'd been listening at the door. What was it about an emergency, I wondered, that brought out the best in some people and the worst in others? I was certain about one thing. As the day progressed, I would encounter both.

Chapter Thirteen

Chief Rivera had received a call and left, but not before taking everyone's names and receiving assurances of their cooperation. He did not inform them of Woody's death, and I asked Olga not to say anything until we were sure Woody's son, Philip, had been notified through official channels. I didn't want Philip to discover that his father was dead in the same way Olga had found out that the ransom was a million dollars.

While the Fishers put her luggage in their van, Olga took a moment to thank her guests and to give Maria Elena last-minute instructions before driving off to the airport in León. With the focus of their attention gone, people got up to leave.

Sarah Christopher pulled me aside. "If today is any indication, this is going to turn into a three-ring circus," she said, shooting a look at the crowd over her shoulder. "I have to run home to take care of a few things. If you want to get away for a few hours, my place is just a short walk from here."

"I appreciate the offer," I said.

"I'll be back later."

"There's no need, Sarah," I said. "Maria Elena and I can manage."

Her face turned stern. "Don't turn down help, Jessica. I'll be back this afternoon."

A short, round man who'd been standing right behind Sarah stepped forward. "Mrs. Fletcher, we didn't have an opportunity to meet. I'm Rafael Sampaio, from the mayor's office," he said, shaking my hand. "The mayor wants to express his great horror that such a terrible thing has happened in San Miguel and to assure you, and of course Mrs. Buckley, that we are cooperating with the police and will do whatever is in our power to make sure Mr. Buckley is brought home safely. This is most upsetting to the mayor. Nothing like this has ever happened before."

"It's kind of you to come, Señor Sampaio."

"I'm afraid I cannot stay any longer. Here is my card. You must call if we can assist in any manner."

"Please thank the mayor for us."

I walked him to the door and stood there while others took their leave.

"We're Ted and Eunice," a small lady said, introducing herself and her husband. "If you need anything, anything at all, Maria Elena has our number."

"We appreciate that."

"Mrs. Fletcher, I was hoping to get to meet you, but not

under these circumstances, of course. I run one of the local bookstores. Perhaps we can talk another time."

"Another time."

"We're in the book," a tall man said, pushing his wife ahead of him. "Call any time, night or day, and we'll be here."

"Thank you," I said, realizing that he'd neglected to give his name.

The Kovachs were the last to go. Nancy stood in front of the hall mirror and adjusted her scarf. "Woody must really want Vaughan to publish his book."

"Why do you say that?" I asked.

"He never put off a trip to accommodate Guy. 'The mail must go through,' he always says."

"He's not a bad sort," Guy said, shaking my hand. "And Vaughan's a good man. Hope they find them both soon."

"You don't have to call on Dina and Roberto," his wife said. "They live out of town. I'm much closer if you need anything. Maria Elena has my number."

"That's very kind," I said, "but I'm sure we'll be fine."

As I closed the door behind them, I overheard Nancy say, "The Fishers always push their way into everyone's lives. You'd think Vaughan was his brother the way Roberto was carrying on. He doesn't even like the man."

I left the door open a crack to hear Guy's reply: "Fisher likes the reflected glory," he said. "Spices up his boring life."

When I returned to the living room, Cathie was helping clear away the glasses and plates while Eric put the borrowed chairs back where they belonged. I picked up the last plate and napkin and followed her down the hall. Maria Elena had given up trying to shoo them away and stood at the sink washing dishes.

"Thank you both for staying to help," I said.

"We feel terrible, Jessica," Cathie said, putting a pitcher of milk in the refrigerator. "We've only known the Buckleys for a short time, but we've become good friends. They're lovely people. And Woody is, too."

"If you can think of something we can do," Eric said, "we're here to lend a hand."

"Actually, there is something, Eric," I said. "Chief Rivera mentioned that kidnappers sometimes send their demands by e-mail. With Olga gone, we have no way of knowing if the men who have Vaughan are trying to contact her. Do you know how I can check *their* e-mail?"

"Sure. I set it up for them," Eric said. "Want me to show you now?"

"If you have the time."

He raised his eyebrows at his wife and cocked his head. "Hon?"

"Go ahead," Cathie said. "I'll pick up the kids and meet you at home." She went to Maria Elena, put an arm around the older woman's shoulder, and whispered something to her.

Maria Elena shook her head and wiped tears from her eyes.

Cathie gave her a squeeze and left.

"They have their regular e-mails at home, of course, which they can access from here," Eric said as we climbed the stairs, "but Vaughan uses his for business. So I set up a joint e-mail for them here in Mexico. You'll only need to check one address."

"How would someone learn their e-mail address?" I asked. "I wouldn't know it unless I asked."

"There's a local telephone directory for the expat community," he replied. "It's up to you if you want to include your e-mail address as well as your phone number, but lots of us do."

"Where can I get a copy?"

"I'm sure there's one downstairs."

Eric pulled the wireless keyboard from its shelf, sat on the sofa, reached for one of the remotes, and pressed buttons. The doors covering the big-screen television slid open and the screen came to life. He patted the place beside him. "Sit here," he said. "It's easy. I'll show you everything."

I watched as he typed in commands on the keyboard, turning the TV into a computer screen.

"This e-mail program has an address book, a calendar, and the usual folders for storing old mail, new mail, and keeping track of mail you've sent. I'll write it out for you," he said, "but once we go over it a few times, it'll be second nature to you."

"Do I need to know their password?"

"No. It's programmed into the computer. Just double-click on this icon and it comes up automatically."

"I don't need to go on the Internet first?"

"Nope," he said, concentrating on the screen. "Doesn't look like there's anything here. Just an announcement of a local concert and an old message from Woody about their upcoming trip." He closed the e-mail window. "This is how you shut it down."

Eric set aside the remotes I was to use and pointed out labels Vaughan had affixed that explained the functions. We went over the instructions a few times until I was confident that I understood the procedure and could find and open their e-mail.

"I hope the cops find these guys before they have a chance to collect any ransom," he said as we went downstairs.

"Me, too," I said. I thanked him again and walked him to the door, intending to go back upstairs to the media room to pull up Woody's e-mail to Vaughan. But the telephone rang. I hurried to the kitchen, where Maria Elena had picked up the receiver, her eyes wide, fear in her face. She listened for a moment and shook her head at me, said a few words and hung up.

I let go a breath I hadn't realized I was holding.

"It is someone from the television station in Mexico City," she said. "I told her we are not talking to the news. *¡Ningún comentario!*"

"No comment," I said, smiling.

The phone rang again. Another reporter was told "*¡Ningún comentario!*"

"We have already seven calls from reporters. See? I write down their names." She held up a pad she'd placed near the telephone. "But nothing from the *bandidos*."

"Perhaps they're waiting to see what the other newspapers print," I said. "You may want to write down the telephone numbers of the reporters in case Olga does want to comment when she gets back."

"*Bueno.* I will do that," she said. "Are you ready for *la comida*? I am making empanadas and a stew for us, and for whoever will come."

"Give me a few minutes," I said. "I have a little more to do on the computer."

I went back upstairs to look at Vaughan's e-mail from Woody, but kept an ear cocked for the ring of the phone. The sound held both hope and frustration. The press was going to be persistent, but we couldn't refuse to answer the phone if there was any possibility that the kidnappers would try to make contact.

I pulled up Woody's e-mail. It was a simple message, merely the time he would be at the house to pick up Vaughan and a suggestion to bring along cash to pay for the gas and for "tips"; the quotation marks were Woody's. His P.S. said, "Don't back out on me, buddy. I'm counting on you."

I opened another folder to see if there was anything helpful in earlier mail Vaughan had saved, and I discovered that the Buckleys had used e-mail to extend the invitations to the party they'd hosted for me. Instead of e-mailing the entire group of people all at once, they had divided the task, each taking a portion of their invitation list and sending personalized messages.

The Fishers' response had been terse, merely saying that they would be happy to attend. Woody's RSVP was more effusive, telling Olga he could never resist any request she made but that Philip unfortunately had previous plans. From my one brief exposure to Philip in front of the police station, I imagined the Manheim men were happy to go their own separate ways when the opportunity arose. Sarah Christopher's reply was predictably flirtatious. I wondered if she thought her words were for Vaughan's eyes only or if she enjoyed the idea that Olga might see her message and read more into their acquaintance than was actually the case.

Maria Elena hovered by the door to the media room, waiting for me to notice her, but I was engrossed in reading the Buckleys' e-mail.

"Señora Fletcher," she called out, "I have made lunch. Would you like me to bring it to you on a tray?"

"Oh, excuse me, Maria Elena," I said. "I didn't realize you were there. No need to bring lunch up. I'll be down in a few minutes. You go ahead without me."

It occurred to me she might be uncomfortable watching me invade her employers' privacy. She might wonder whether Olga would be angry with her if she found out. After all, Maria Elena was responsible for the house and all its contents. The Buckleys trusted her. Yet here was a guest not just looking to see if there was a message from the kidnappers but delving into their private correspondence and personal messages. Was she worried about losing her job, which would also mean losing her home? I resolved to put her mind at ease at the first possible moment.

Olga had asked me to stay to deal with the police and to

field messages from the kidnappers should they try to communicate with her. I considered that I was "on the case" and meant to apply whatever instincts and talents I had on her behalf and Vaughan's. If that meant reading their mail, interviewing their friends, and delving into intimate matters they might not be so eager to have exposed, so be it. We were pursuing criminals. Vaughan's life was in jeopardy. This was not a time for niceties.

I opened the calendar—it was empty—looked for a record of documents that had been viewed recently, and opened one called "JBF party invitations." It contained the names and e-mail addresses of all the people the Buckleys had invited to the cocktail party, together with a column of check marks next to those who'd been expected to attend. I printed it out. It was doubtful that everyone at the gathering knew about the mail run, but I would give the list to Chief Rivera if he thought it would be helpful.

The chief had said the kidnapping wasn't a spur-of-the-moment attack, that it would have been planned in advance. How many people knew when Woody and Vaughan were going on the mail run and when they would be returning? Probably all the families with post office boxes in Laredo and at least a few of the people I'd met at the party. I made a mental list of those who could provide some answers, including Maria Elena.

I also needed to pay a visit to the editor of *Noticias*. Exactly when had he received that note about the ransom? Philip was on my list as well. Woody's son might be able to fill in some gaps in my information. After that, I'd have to see. Not speaking Spanish was going to limit my ability to investigate. But there might be ways around that. I had overcome language barriers before. I hoped I could do it again, in time to save my publisher and friend.

I closed the document with the names of the party attendees and also closed the list of e-mail messages. The computer made a loud dinging noise. I pulled my fingers from the keyboard as if they'd been scorched. *What did I do?* I thought, looking down at the keys. Had I inadvertently pressed a wrong key? I looked up and a chill skittered along my spine, raising goose bumps on my arms. A small box filled the center of the screen.

"*Hola,* Señora Buckley," it said. "We have your husband."

Chapter Fourteen

Chief Rivera was not at his desk when I called, but he was expected back later in the afternoon.

The kidnappers had made contact, but our exchange had not been productive. When I realized the little box was an instant message, I had jotted down the name of the sender, "Pelican," clicked on the REPLY button, and typed in, "Is Vaughan all right?"

The message came back immediately: "The ransom is one million dollars American."

"Please allow Vaughan to call home so I may hear his voice," I wrote.

"We will tell you where to leave the money."

I typed back: "I must have proof that Vaughan is alive and unharmed."

"You will receive instructions tomorrow."

"Tell me! Is he all right?"

There were no more messages.

I shook my head in frustration. It was as if they didn't understand what I was writing, as if they had a preplanned message and that was all I was going to get.

Pelican. A bird. Was there any significance to the name? SMA is landlocked. Why did the revolutionaries choose to use the name of a seabird? Did the sea represent freedom to them?

I reached for the phone and dialed Olga's cell phone number. She would be in the air by now, but I'd promised to call right away. I left a brief message that the kidnappers had made contact, that I would learn more tomorrow, and that I would call again later. I went downstairs to tell Maria Elena.

"I am at your disposal," she said. "Señora Buckley, she asked that I help you in any way that I can. The house is open to you."

I had expressed to Maria Elena my concern that she might be reluctant to allow me access to the Buckleys' private correspondence, explaining that I hoped something I saw might hold a clue as to Vaughan's captors or his whereabouts.

"Whatever I know, I give to you with my whole heart," she said.

We sat at the kitchen table with the local telephone directory, a map of San Miguel de Allende, and a pad of paper. Between answering phone calls, we were making lists of who might have known about Woody and Vaughan's trip and writing down directions to help me find my way around town. Now that the kidnappers had communi-

cated, after a fashion, I didn't need to stay home to wait for
their call. I was free to follow leads of my own.

"I do not talk about Señor and Señora Buckley to anyone," she said. "Not even to my brother, unless it is to tell
him he is needed for some work. But Señor Buckley, he is
so excited to go, he talks about it to everyone."

"I was afraid of that," I said.

"I hear him on the telephone with Señor Woody making
plans. His voice is like a young man," she said, smiling at the
memory. "They plan to go three times and have to change
their minds, but then they finally make the date this week."

"Why did they postpone the trip before?" I asked.

"Señora Buckley, she did not want him to go. Twice he
makes the appointment and she talks him out of it. Once,
because you come, and he would not think to leave and not
be here to welcome you."

"Does Vaughan have a desk that he uses? I didn't see
one in the media room."

"In the living room, from an antique store in New York
City. I will show it to you."

I didn't remember there being a desk in the living room
and soon discovered why.

Maria Elena lifted a heavy ceramic jug from the carved
Spanish chest next to the fireplace and swept away the embroidered cloth that had protected the top, depositing both
on the glass coffee table. She pulled open the doors that
formed the front panel of the chest and lifted the lid, revealing drawers on either side, an open space between, and
a recessed desktop with horizontal slots for papers.

"I'm learning more about Vaughan on this trip than in all the years I've known him," I said. "It seems he likes to hide things behind closed doors."

"The señora says she does not want him to do business while they are here."

"So, he buys a desk that doesn't look like a desk," I said.

"If you need anything else, please call for me," she said, leaving to answer the phone.

The desk drawers were mostly empty, with only a few pens and pencils, some flyers for local events, and his checkbook. Blank sheets of paper and envelopes filled the narrow slots, but under the blotter I found what I was looking for—a calendar page for the month. The date of the mail run was marked in pencil, as was the day of my expected arrival in San Miguel. There were two places where entries had been erased, presumably the previously planned trips that Vaughan had put off.

The phone rang again. Maria Elena's list of press calls was up to fifteen.

The offices of *Noticias* were in a small building off El Jardin, having moved from their previous location on the outskirts of town. Computers had been hooked up and the copier plugged in, but boxes stacked against two walls had yet to be unpacked, and from the looks of the desk of the editor, Guillermo Sylva, I guessed they might never be. Piles of newspapers, magazines, catalogs, and papers littered his workspace. It was a wonder he ever found anything he was looking for.

"I told you, Señora Fletcher—I gave the note to the police. They were on my doorstep when I came in this morning."

"I'm not surprised, Señor Sylva. It seems you may have known about the kidnapping before anyone else did."

He grinned. "I had to remake the whole front page. I was up till three with the printer. But we got the story in, and published on time. No one can say *Noticias* doesn't cover the hard news."

"Do you have a large staff?"

He pointed at his chest. "I'm the reporter, editor, and publisher," he said, "but I get help from volunteer stringers."

"The newspaper is a weekly, isn't it?"

He gave a sharp nod.

"You'll pardon me if I say so, Señor Sylva, and I don't mean to offend you, but I had the distinct impression that *Noticias* was more of a social newspaper, one that gives greater focus to calendar items like concerts and art exhibits and to real estate listings than to hard news."

"That criticism has been leveled before, Señora Fletcher, but it's not true. I attended journalism school in the States. It's why the new owners hired me, and why I convinced them to open an office closer to the center of action. We're working hard to counter those critics, to be a full-service newspaper, to cover all the news, while at the same time keeping what our loyal readership wants."

"And what your loyal advertisers want," I added.

"Of course," he said. "Or we'd be out of business."

"It must be difficult competing with daily news outlets when you publish only once a week."

"Difficult, but not impossible. We try to take a different tack, find a new angle, do a news analysis or come up with some interesting sidebar the other media haven't picked up on yet."

"But not this time."

"It's not often I can scoop the Mexico City dailies and the online papers that cover SMA, but this time it was a doozy." He fiddled with a paper on his desk and looked at me out of the corner of his eye. "Of course, they'll beat me to the news of Señor Manheim's death." He raised his head. "I see you're not surprised. That's interesting. I heard it on the scanner this morning. How did you find out?"

I ignored his question and asked another of my own. "Why do you suppose the kidnappers chose you to publish their demands, rather than another paper?"

He shrugged. "Maybe because we're the only official paper in SMA. The others are from out of town. They know all the expats read *Noticias*. That way the families of the victims would be able to read about their demands."

"Wouldn't it be more logical for them to contact the families first, before they sent their demands to you?"

"Maybe they did," he said, picking up a pen and twirling it between his fingers.

"You know they didn't," I said. "Mrs. Buckley received a call from *Noticias* last night. That was you, wasn't it? I thought it was an odd time to call about a subscription."

"I was going to try to get a comment from her about the kidnapping, but when she said her husband would be home later, I realized she didn't know."

"Then the note mentioned Vaughan by name?"

He nodded slowly. "Both of them. Manheim and Buckley."

"And you didn't inform Mrs. Buckley about it."

"I wasn't about to tell her that her husband had been kidnapped. No! That's a job for the cops, not me."

"Did you try to corroborate that the note was genuine?"

"I knew the cops had found an abandoned car. I heard it on the scanner. I knew it was a gringo car. Part of the description was a sign in the window saying the driver doesn't speak Spanish."

"Perhaps the revolutionaries heard about it on the scanner, too. Maybe they took credit for something they didn't do."

"Maybe. But then how would they know the names of the two men?"

"I don't know," I said, "but something isn't right. I'm told that the local revolutionary group is more interested in making political statements than in committing crimes."

"Kidnapping two Americans is a heck of a statement, don't you think? Look, Señora Fletcher, there are revolutionary groups active all over this country. The powers that be can't keep up with them. Quash 'em over here, they pop up over there. As long as there's corruption in the government and in the legal and judicial systems—and that's still the case, despite the best efforts of those in the current administration—the rebel groups have a reason to go on. Maybe our local revolutionaries just figured it was time to take a bolder stand, make a bigger splash."

"Maybe so," I said. "May I see the note?"

"I told you, the police took it."

"A sharp editor like yourself, Señor Sylva, would have made a copy of the note, knowing the police would demand the original."

What came from him was more a bark than a laugh. "You're pretty sharp yourself," he said, taking a key from his pocket, unlocking one of his desk drawers, and pulling out a file folder. "Would you like a copy of it?"

"That would be very helpful," I said. "I don't suppose you've heard from them again?"

"Not yet," he said, getting up and turning on the copier, "but I wouldn't be surprised if I did." He took a sheet of paper from the folder.

"What's that mark on the corner?" I asked.

"Just an ink smudge."

"Did you make it or was it on the original?"

"Not me. I don't use a fountain pen. By the way, is there a reward?"

"Not so far. I think Mrs. Buckley will want to ask the police if they think it's a good idea first. We don't want to do anything to jeopardize Vaughan's position."

"It'd make a difference. People will come forward with all kinds of information if they think there's something in it for them."

"Are you including yourself?"

"No way. The board would never let me accept a reward." He waited while the copy machine warmed up. "Listen, I'm doing you a favor," he said. "How about doing one for me?"

"What can I do?" I asked.

"I'd like to interview you for the paper, Señora Fletcher. We have a lot of authors in town, but none who're famous for solving crimes. Plus, you're a friend of the victim. That gives you a unique perspective. I want an exclusive, nothing the other papers can get. Give it to me and I'll even share any information that comes my way."

"What information do you think you'd get?"

"You never know. San Miguel is a lot like a small town. It's hard to keep secrets here. If someone knows what you're doing, he'll tell somebody else. And that person will tell another. Word gets around. And when it does, it sometimes comes to me."

"I'll make a deal with you, Señor Sylva. You share information that helps me find Vaughan Buckley, and I'll present myself at this office for an exclusive interview."

He smiled and put the paper in the copy machine. "Okay, but there's more."

"What else do you want?" I asked.

"I want to sit down with Señor Buckley. I want to learn what happened in his own words, a blow-by-blow description. I really want to talk with him."

"So do I, Señor Sylva. So do I."

Chapter Fifteen

The police station was only a short distance from the newspaper office, and I walked there after my visit with the editor, taking a shortcut through El Jardin. The park was small as parks go, and after a few visits its features were beginning to look familiar: the gazebo; the children skipping and chasing each other; the benches filled with people, newcomers and natives alike, reading, chatting, snoozing in the shade of the tall laurel trees.

My eyes scanned El Jardin looking for a bouquet of balloons that would indicate the balloon vendor was there again. I'd become increasingly convinced that he was the man who had robbed me the night I came to San Miguel de Allende. The balloon vendor was thinner than my assailant had been, but I recalled that the *bandido* had looked as if he were wearing layers of clothing. Take them away and you take pounds off his appearance. The cough, of course, was the giveaway. Not that everyone with a cough could be considered under suspicion.

A little girl, no more than two years old, ran up to me and wrapped her arms around my knees, squealing with delight. She was wearing a cotton dress, too large for her slight frame, the fabric thin from many washings and the hem frayed.

"Hello," I said. "Who are you?"

She grinned back at an older boy of about five, who was chasing her. Releasing my knees, she darted behind me, and the two children ran in circles, the baby using my body as a shield. I heard a man's shout and the pair of imps ran away, the little one laughing and waving at me. I smiled and waved back, enjoying the youngsters' exuberance, their innocent enjoyment of a simple game.

I sometimes wonder how different my life would have been if Frank and I had had children. It was never our intention to be childless. We started our marriage with every expectation that our lives would mirror those of our friends and family. It just didn't turn out that way. At first we were consumed with our failure, jealous of others' easy fertility, angry at our inability to accomplish something everyone around us was capable of doing: producing offspring. But as the years passed we made peace with our disappointment, settled into a comfortable routine, and found our joy elsewhere, in sweet times together, listening, learning, loving. I have no regrets. We had a tender and close relationship, one I cherish in memory.

Musing on the ironies life presents, I walked to the corner with the ice cream stand and waited for traffic to subside. It was late in the day, and the tourist buses were returning to

the park, jockeying for position at the curb to let their passengers off. One bus came so close to where I stood I had to
take a step back to avoid being hit by the side mirror.

What happened next took place in an instant. The little
girl raced to the corner and turned to taunt her brother,
dancing backward toward the street. Her tiny sandal caught
in the curb and she tumbled into the gutter just as a bus
was pulling out. I heard screams but never stopping to
think, I ran in front of the bus—its horn blaring—scooped
up the child, and jumped back onto the sidewalk. I was sur-
rounded by people, cheering me, all talking at once, pounding me on the back. The little girl was frightened by the
commotion and began to cry. She reached her arms out to
her father. I delivered her to him and looked up into his
tearful eyes. It was the balloon vendor.

I found Chief Rivera on the telephone, leaning back in
his chair with his feet up on the desk. He wore his Yankees
baseball cap backward, the bill turned around to the nape
of his neck. He waved me to a seat and finished his conversation.

"We found the gun," he said, dropping his feet to the
floor and hanging up the phone.

"The gun that killed Woody?"

"Yeah." He took off the cap and ran a hand over the top
of his crew cut. "I was just talking to the ballistics guy over
in Guanajuato. Says it looks like it might match the bullet
the coroner pulled from the vic—uh, Mr. Manheim's body.
We're waiting for the confirmation."

"That was quick," I said.

"Sometimes we can be efficient," he said with a small smile.

"Where did you find it?"

"The gun? About thirty feet from the body, in some brush. Can't believe we missed it this morning."

"Strange that the kidnappers wouldn't keep it."

"I agree."

"Will you be able to trace the gun?" I asked. "Is there any chance it was registered?"

"The serial number wasn't scratched off, so we lucked out there," he said. "No record of registration in Mexico, however."

"In that case," I said, "it must be illegal. I understand the Mexican government has strict rules when it comes to firearms."

"You understand correctly. You get caught with an un-registered weapon, they can put you away for thirty years, no questions asked. That's not to say there aren't a lot of contraband arms floating around. They pour over the border. This may be one of them, but we've got to wait to find out. I've got the basic data going to ATF in the States, just to cover all bases," he said, referring to the Bureau of Alcohol, Tobacco, Firearms, and Explosives, which keeps track of registered weapons."

"What kind of gun is it?"

"Beretta nine-millimeter pistol."

"A gun like that is standard military issue back home," I said. "Did you find any fingerprints?"

"We got two full and a partial. Nothing back yet." He held up two hands as if to ward me off. "Mrs. Fletcher, I've told you all I can. Why don't you leave the rest of this investigation to us?"

"The kidnappers are demanding a ransom," I said.

"It was only a matter of time. How did they contact you?"

"An instant message on the computer."

"That's new."

I shook my head. "It was lucky I was online at the time; otherwise I would have missed them." I told the chief about the sender's name, the lack of response to my queries about Vaughan, and my hunch that they were simply delivering a prepared statement.

"Could be. They probably don't speak English. They've already botched their mission and lost one piece of bait, possibly both. They could be bluffing."

"What do you make of the name Pelican?" I asked.

"Don't know. It's a bird that can carry a lot of fish in its beak. Maybe it's a symbol of some sort."

"That's what I was thinking, but a symbol of what?"

"You can't always figure these things," he said. "Some people like to be obscure, play with your mind. It gives them a kick."

"I guess. Do you mind if I ask you a question?" I said.

He started to laugh.

"What's so funny?" I asked.

"You've already asked me a hundred questions," he said, throwing up his hands. "What's one more? I wish my staff were as hot on the case as you are."

"I don't mean to interfere," I said. "I just want Vaughan Buckley found unharmed."

His face became serious. "We have the same objective, but you do realize it doesn't look good with one already dead."

"You've had men up in the mountains all day without finding any trace of Mr. Buckley. Am I right?"

He looked at his watch. "Haven't heard from the pilot yet. The helicopter might still be searching the area. We won't get the dog till day after tomorrow, the earliest."

"If I don't miss my guess," I said, "they won't find him there. At least they won't find his body."

"How can you be so sure?"

"The vultures. They discover a corpse a lot faster than a helicopter. We saw only two birds, and they were both fixated on Woody."

"I hope for your friend's sake that you're right."

I gave Chief Rivera the guest list from the party and explained that I had downloaded it from Vaughan's computer. "I don't know how helpful that will be," I said, "but I thought you should have it."

He put the papers in the top file on his desk. "You never know when some piece of information will prove useful," he said, standing and stretching. "It's been a long day. I'm going home for supper. Would you like a lift back to the Buckleys' house?"

"Oh, that would be very nice of you. Thanks."

We walked down the hall to the magnetic board that displayed police personnel and patrols. Rivera moved a disk with his name to the off-duty slot. At the bottom of the stairwell a small contingent of soldiers was loitering in the vestibule, as if awaiting instructions. Chief Rivera didn't speak again until we were outside and away from the building. "Their major has been chewing nails all day," he said. "The Revolutionary Guanajuato Brigade has eluded him several times, but this is the first time they've gotten him in trouble."

"So he's tried to find them before?" I asked.

"He didn't put a lot of effort into it. The members of the brigade, such as it is, apparently move around, don't stay in one place for very long."

"If I remember correctly, you thought they were harmless. 'Three men and a copier,' you said."

"Up until now they never did anything other than issue these inflammatory proclamations, you know, calls to rise up against the government, that sort of thing. It was enough to put them on a Wanted list but not enough to warrant an all-out campaign to stamp them out. Now the feds are holding the major's feet to the fire, wanting to know why his soldiers haven't hauled them in before."

We walked around the corner and down several streets, stopping at a wide archway sealed by solid wooden panels. Chief Rivera took out a large key, unbolted the doors, pushed them back, and kicked a stone in front of each to hold it open. I followed him into an unevenly paved square where a dozen police and unmarked vehicles were haphazardly parked. He opened the passenger door of a gleaming black sedan, and I got in.

I put on the seat belt and waited for him to come around the car. "Something is bothering me," I said when he was settled in the driver's seat.

"What's that?"

"Doesn't it strike you as odd that previously peaceful demonstrators have suddenly turned violent?"

"It would, except they put the statement in the paper demanding ransom and knew the names of the missing men."

"Speaking of that ransom demand, did you know about that this morning when we went to the scene of the crime?"

He snorted. "I wondered when you were going to ask me that."

"Why didn't you say anything?"

"I don't share all my secrets with you, Mrs. Fletcher. Sometimes you learn more by keeping quiet than by speaking."

"I'll assume I was among your suspects, then," I said. "Am I still under suspicion?"

"I don't cross anyone off till I've made an arrest. But you're far down on my list, at least for the moment."

"That's comforting."

He started up the engine, left the car idling on the street while he relocked the doors to the parking area, and got back behind the wheel.

"How long do you figure Mrs. Buckley will be away?" he asked as we bounced over the cobblestones.

"She didn't say," I replied, "but I doubt it will be more than a few days. She'll want to be here when Vaughan is released."

"You're an optimist."

"I have to be. I can't conceive of anything else. Vaughan Buckley and I have been colleagues and friends for more years than I care to count. If these people are holding him for ransom, they're going to have to produce him before any money changes hands."

"Under the circumstances, I'd say they're the ones setting the rules."

"We'll see," I said. "Have they gotten in touch with Philip Manheim?"

"He claims they haven't. I saw him this afternoon for about ten minutes. We sent a priest with the officers to give him the news. Weird kid. Seemed more angry than sad at the loss of his father. And his friends looked like something out of a gang war movie. Toughs with an attitude. D'you know him? The kid, I mean?"

"I've met him, but we've never had so much as a conversation. I wasn't impressed with his manners. But young people are sometimes like that around their parents' acquaintances."

"I'm keeping an eye on him. He left the house right after I did and, according to my guys, hasn't been back since."

"He has a lot to deal with right now," I said. "Maybe he went to stay with friends. It can be painful to be alone when someone you love dies."

"I don't know how much love there was between them."

"Sometimes it isn't obvious to the casual observer," I said, "but that doesn't mean it doesn't exist."

"I guess you're right. I'm going to swing by his house if you don't mind. News media were staked out on the street earlier. Even a couple of TV crews. I'm hoping they're gone by now."

"How awful for him. I can certainly understand why Philip would want to leave."

He drove to a part of town I hadn't walked through yet, the streets narrower and not quite so picturesque as the one on which Vaughan and Olga lived. I knew which building was Woody's by the tilted TV remote van parked outside, two wheels up on the sidewalk to keep it out of the way of any traffic. On top was a huge telescoping antenna; it looked as if it might make the truck topple over at any moment.

Chief Rivera pulled a bubble light from under his seat, rolled down the window, and slapped it on his hood. He plugged the cord into the cigarette lighter and I saw the reflection of the beam on the building.

"I'm going in to see if he's back," he said, opening the door.

"Do you mind if I join you?" I asked, releasing my seat belt.

His raised eyebrows hinted that he was going to object, but instead he said, "Suit yourself."

I followed him into the small courtyard of Woody's building. It was apparent that more than one family lived there. Stone staircases to the right and left led to upstairs entrances. Laundry was strung on a rope from one of the upper apartments to the wall across from it. Two doors were at ground level behind the stairs. A man with a camera on his shoulder was filming another man who stood before one of them, which I assumed was the entrance to where Woody had lived.

The reporter finished talking and lowered his microphone, and the cameraman flipped off the bright light attached to his equipment.

Rivera flashed his badge and asked the reporter something in Spanish.

"If he's in there, we never saw him," the man replied in English.

"Wrapping up now? I don't want that truck blocking the street."

"We have to transmit the feed, but we'll be gone in ten minutes."

The door to Woody's apartment was unlocked. I didn't know if Philip had forgotten to lock it or if he always left it open, as many of my neighbors do at home—despite Mort Metzger, our sheriff in Cabot Cove, strongly discouraging that custom. He always says it's an unfortunate fact of twenty-first-century life that we live in times too dangerous to allow anyone to walk in unannounced. It saddens me that the innocent days of trusting the good intentions of neighbor and stranger alike are gone. Nevertheless, I recognize the truth of that and have regretfully followed Mort's advice. I lock my doors even when I'm home.

Chief Rivera knocked on the door and called out "Anybody home?" before he swung it open and entered one end of a short room. Woody's apartment was cramped and dim. A single lamp had been left lit, but it did little to illuminate the dark corners and massive furniture that crowded the center of the space. It took a few minutes for my eyes to adjust to the gloom, but it was apparent that Woody and his son kept the place neat, except for a pile of magazines that sat on a coffee table in front of a well-worn, overstuffed leather sofa. A serape that was usually tucked under the cushion covered the seat, but one side had come loose, revealing a crack in the leather. Woody had been a large man, and his furniture reflected his size. A pair of matching armchairs flanked the sofa, all three pieces facing a television set that sat on a rough wooden table against the wall, next to a computer monitor.

I touched Rivera's arm and pointed to the computer. "Philip might have e-mail that could tell us where he went," I said.

"I'm within my rights to come in and see if he's here, but I don't have a search warrant, and I'm not about to start stretching the law. He's not missing yet. We just want to talk with him again."

"He could be out making arrangements for the funeral," I offered. "When will you release the body?"

"Not till I get the results of the autopsy."

Four doors led off the living room. I followed the chief as he poked his head in the kitchen and pushed open the bathroom door. There were two bedrooms, and it was easy to see who belonged in each one. Woody's was spare and neat, a testament to his years in the military. His bed was made, and the only item on his dresser was a small tray for coins and other contents of his pockets. Philip's room was plastered with posters of rock bands and buxom movie starlets. His bed, a mattress on the floor, was a pile of grubby linen. Clothes had been dropped and left where they landed. I wouldn't have been surprised to see a teenager's room look like this, but Philip was already out of his teens. His sloppiness must have galled his father, and maybe that was his intent. Or perhaps it was just the absence of a feminine presence to shame him into cleaning it up.

"Kid's a slob," Chief Rivera said. "He'd never get away with that in my house."

"I wonder why he still lived with his father," I said.

"Probably couldn't find work. The government doesn't want foreigners taking jobs a Mexican can do."

"Do you know if his mother is living?"

"I didn't do the interview," he said. "Gutierrez will probably know."

On our way out, I caught sight of a picture near the entrance that I hadn't noticed earlier when my eyes were adjusting to the lack of light. It was a Sarah Christopher painting from what I now thought of as her "revolutionary" period. It showed several figures arming themselves for battle. One of them, a woman, looked familiar. I moved closer to the picture and squinted up at the face. Her features were contorted from the effort needed to lift a heavy sword, but one thing was unmistakably clear: The picture was a self-portrait of the artist.

Chapter Sixteen

Wonderful cooking aromas filled the house when I arrived back at the Buckleys' after Chief Rivera dropped me off. I found Maria Elena at the stove and her brother sitting at the kitchen table. Their faces were somber, and there were traces of tears on her cheeks. Hector hastily scrambled to his feet when I walked through the door. I knew at once they had learned about Woody.

"Such sad news about Señor Woody, Señora Fletcher," Maria Elena said, wiping her eyes. "We hear it on the radio."

"I'm so sorry you had to learn about it that way," I said. "The police asked me not to say anything until they spoke with his son."

"Does Señora Buckley know? It will be terrible to tell her."

"Yes. She knows."

"Poor Philipo," she said. "His papa was such a nice man. He always compliments me on my cooking. I'm making some food to send to the boy. Do you think that will be all right? It is our custom."

"I'm sure he'll appreciate it even if he doesn't say so right away. If you like, I can bring it to him this evening when I go there. I'll be sure to tell him you made it for him."

"That would be most kind." She gestured toward her brother. "*Dispénseme*," she said. "Señora, this is my brother Hector. He works for Señor Buckley sometimes."

Hector bobbed his head to me. "I helped to repair the house for them," he said.

"Mr. Buckley has spoken very highly of you," I said. "It's a pleasure to meet you."

"I think highly of him as well or I wouldn't want my sister to come work here."

Maria Elena frowned at him. "Be nice."

"It's true," he said looking at her. "You are my responsibility now. I don't entrust you to just anyone."

"He is just leaving, Señora," she said.

"Please don't leave on my account," I said. "In fact, I'll join you for a few minutes, if you don't mind." I pulled out a chair and sat. "Please sit down," I said to Hector.

He took the chair opposite mine, a wary expression in his eyes.

Maria Elena wrung her hands, worried that her brother would be rude to her houseguest. He was a proud man, and a bit of a hothead. I'd seen that side of him at the Buckleys' party when he'd stormed out of the kitchen, but I wasn't concerned. I had an idea I wanted to discuss. The editor of *Noticias* had said San Miguel was like a small town, where rumors and gossip spread quickly. He was going to keep his ears open, but his readership was mostly in the expatriate community. Hector might be able to track down rumors circulating among the Mexican residents.

"I'd like to ask your help in finding Mr. Buckley," I said.

Whatever he thought I was going to say, this wasn't it. His face registered surprise, then anger. "I have nothing to do with this crime," he said, jumping up. "I would never hurt Mr. Buckley."

"I think you misunderstand," I said. "I simply thought that since you live here, you might be able to find out some information."

"You ask me this because I am Mexican? You Americans assume we are all alike. Everyone is not to be trusted. Even in our own country, you accuse us of trying to cheat you."

"I'm not accusing you of anything," I said, feeling myself getting heated as well. "On the contrary, if you let me finish, you'll realize I'm asking for your assistance. Vaughan Buckley needs all the help we can provide." I sat back and shook my head. "But if you can't control your temper any better than that, I doubt we can get very far. I don't want to make circumstances any more difficult for Vaughan than they already are."

Maria Elena released a furious stream of Spanish at her brother.

He looked at her sheepishly and sank back down in his seat. "*Lo siento mucho, Señora.* I am sorry to interrupt you. Of course I want to help Señor Buckley. What is it I can do for him?"

I took a breath and said, "You can listen. That's all I'm asking. Just listen."

"I am listening," he said.

I shook my head. "That's not what I mean," I said, thinking, *I must be tired. I can't even express myself clearly anymore.* "I talked with the editor of *Noticias* today," I continued. "He said San Miguel is like a small town, where it is hard to keep a secret. People talk."

Both Hector and Maria Elena nodded.

"It seems to me it would be difficult to hide a kidnap victim in San Miguel, particularly a tall American, without someone hearing or seeing something. What you can do is simply offer opportunities for information. If you're with a group of people, in a shop or in church or at work, talk about the kidnapping and see if anyone has any theories about who might be responsible."

"The police are already asking questions," Hector said. "They were down at the market talking with the people."

"Sometimes people are hesitant to talk with the police," I said. "That's why there's a possibility you might learn something that they can't."

Maria Elena cleared her throat. "I could bring my washing to the *lavandería* at El Chorro," she said. "There is a lot of talk there."

"Exactly!" Olga had taken me to see the communal laundry across from Parque Benito Juárez when we'd spent the morning playing tourist. "That's a brilliant idea," I said.

She beamed.

"I can ask at the cantina," Hector said. "The men at the

bar, they always talk about politics and crime and their bosses."

"Wonderful," I said. "But be careful. You don't want to raise suspicions or make yourself a target."

"Tomorrow I will go down to the garden center where the men, they wait for landscaping work."

"Another good place," I said.

"And I will tell Father Alfredo. He knows everyone. I will do it," he said, thumping his fist on the table and standing. "I start tonight."

"Thank you both," I said.

"And Señora Fletcher," he said, "I am sorry to yell at you. Sometimes, it is difficult—"

"I understand," I said, interrupting him. "It's all forgotten."

"*Gracias.*"

"Your supper will be ready soon, Señora," Maria Elena said after her brother left. "Would you like some wine or some tea? I have hot water ready."

"Tea would be lovely," I replied. "I'll be in the media room."

I went upstairs and checked Vaughan's e-mail. The kidnappers had said they would contact me the next day, but I wanted to be certain they hadn't changed their mind. While I was there, I read my own e-mail, surfed the Internet for information about Mexican revolutionary groups, and looked to see if there were any stories about pelicans and symbolism. I placed a call to Olga, getting her voice mail once again.

Maria Elena was ladling stew into a large casserole when I returned to the kitchen.

"Thank you for the tea," I said, rinsing the cup at the sink.

"*De nada*," she said. "I have made for Senor Woody's son a *birria*. It is a traditional dish, very filling. I have it for you for dinner as well."

I insisted on eating in the kitchen, although I think Maria Elena would have preferred to serve me in the dining room. I tried Olga once more before I left, but she was either out of range or didn't have her cell phone turned on.

Maria Elena placed the casserole in a box along with corn tortillas wrapped in foil, put the box in a shopping bag for me, and called a cab to take me to Woody's apartment. "Perhaps he can return the pot when he is finished eating."

"I'm sure it won't be a problem," I said.

It didn't look as if Philip had been back since Chief Rivera and I were there earlier. I knocked on the door, and when there was no answer I entered the empty apartment and by the light of the one dim lamp headed straight for the kitchen. I flipped on the overhead fluorescent, unpacked the box with the stew, and found a container to transfer it to so I could take the rinsed pot back to Maria Elena. When I opened the refrigerator to put the stew in, I was pleased to see that others had been there before me. Should Philip come home anytime soon, he would not have to cook for himself for a while.

I think every culture in the world connects death with food. In times of bereavement, when words fail us, it's the only way we know to comfort each other, to *nurture* the people in mourning. When my husband died, my friends and neighbors filled my refrigerator and freezer with all manner of baked goods and casseroles. It was ironic, when you think about it, because it was a time when I had no appetite at all and didn't really want to eat or even to talk to all the visitors who flowed in and out of my home. I wondered if Philip felt the same way, if he had disappeared to avoid all the well-meaning people who came to feed him and to offer their condolences.

I pulled a piece of paper from the spiral notebook in my bag and wrote him a note saying that the stew was from Maria Elena and the Buckleys and expressing their sorrow at his loss. I left it on the kitchen table and turned off the light.

In Philip's bedroom, I opened an armoire that served as both closet and dresser. All his clothing, other than what had been left on the floor, seemed to be there, as well as a backpack and a suitcase that occupied the top shelf. A similar piece of furniture in Woody's room showed signs of his having packed; the top shelf was bare, and several empty hangers dangled in the middle of the rod. Neither man had an extensive wardrobe. They obviously lived modestly on Woody's military pension.

In the living room, I sat on the sofa and looked around, listening to the noises from the apartment upstairs, muffled voices and the cries of a baby, accompanied by music and laughter from the sound track of a program on television.

The one lamp, on the table next to me, cast a circle of

light in the center of the room but left the corners in shadows. The illumination would not be enough to allow comfortable reading, but it was sufficient to make out the titles in the stack of publications on the cocktail table: an assortment of sports-related magazines, one on guns, another on bullfighting, a catalog from a university in the States, another from an auto parts company. I found a copy of *Noticias* with an ad for an art gallery circled. When I picked it up, a postcard fell out from between the pages. It was from a local bookseller informing Woody that his order had arrived and was being held for him. I put it in my bag.

Nothing I'd found in the three rooms gave any hint of where Philip might have gone or when he might return. I eyed the computer. Maybe it held a clue. I pulled a stool out from under the table that held the television and the monitor, turned on the computer, and put my hand on the mouse. The monitor made a buzzing noise and the screen slowly came to life. Following the same directions I'd used for Vaughan's computer, I signed on to Woody's e-mail. Several of the messages were in Spanish. Between the noises from upstairs and my concentration on the screen, I didn't hear the door open.

"Who are you and what are you doing?"

"Good heavens!" I exclaimed, turning and placing a hand over my racing heart. "You startled me, Philip."

"I'll do more than that. I'm going to call the police," he said, squinting at me. "And how do you know my name?" He looked unkempt, with several days' growth of beard and dark crescents under his eyes. His shirt was wrinkled as if he'd slept in it.

"We've met before," I said. "I'm Jessica Fletcher. I'm so sorry about your father."

He seemed at a loss how to respond. "I don't remember meeting you," he said, closing the door behind him. "Are you a friend of my father's?"

"We met the other day, in front of the police station. I was with Olga Buckley."

"Yeah. Okay." He walked to the sofa and threw himself down, closing his eyes.

"I brought you some stew. It's in the refrigerator. Maria Elena, the Buckleys' housekeeper, made it. She was very fond of your father. Would you like me to heat it up for you?"

He shook his head.

"There's other food that people have brought for you."

"Not hungry. Just want to sleep," he mumbled.

"Where have you been?" I asked. "The police were here looking for you."

"Out. I've been out."

"Were you staying with friends?"

"Yeah."

"Who were you staying with?"

"What time is it anyway?" He squinted at his wrist. "I've lost my watch."

"Mine was stolen," I said. "I think it must be around nine o'clock."

"Why were you on my computer?" His voice rose as he fought to stay awake.

"I was trying to see if I could figure out where you were."

"Why? What does it matter? I was there. Now I'm here." His eyes drifted closed again.

"Philip, pay attention. Who knew which day your father was coming home from the mail run?"

He shrugged. "I don't know. Mrs. Buckley must have known, possibly the Fishers. I knew. Maybe a few others. Who cares? It's too late now."

"Why do you say the Fishers would know?" I asked. "Why would he tell them in particular? I thought they didn't have a post office box in Laredo."

"They don't." He rubbed his nose with his hand.

"Philip, stay awake a little longer."

"I'm awake, I'm awake. What did you want to know?"

"The Fishers. Why would Woody tell them when he was returning?"

"Maybe he didn't, but Roberto asked me for the hotel number in Monterrey. He wanted my dad to pick up a few things for him."

"Like what?"

"Stuff. I don't know. He always gave Dad a shopping list. Gotta sleep. Too tired to talk."

"All right. One more question and I'll leave you alone."

"Okay. Just one." He pulled his feet up on the cushion and lay on his back, one arm shielding his eyes from the light of the lamp.

"The day we met, you and Woody were coming out of the police station. What were you doing there?"

"Telling the cops."

"Telling the police what?"

"Uh, uh, uh. That's more than one question." He smiled, but his eyes remained closed.

"What did he tell the police?"

"About the mail run. He told them every time he went."

"Why did he do that?"

"For protection," he said through a yawn. "He said they'd keep an eye on the house. Watch out for him on the road. Like back home, when you go on vacation and let the cops know you'll be gone and stop the mail and the newspapers."

"So he reported his trips to the police?"

He snorted. "Lot of good it did him, huh? They ignored it as usual," he said, his voice trailing off.

"I wonder," I said. But Philip didn't hear me. The sound of his breathing had deepened, his chest rising and falling gently as sleep claimed him.

Chapter Seventeen

"You know, I can see this as the basis of a real murder mystery," Roberto said, reaching for his second corn griddle cake and slathering it with salsa.

He had knocked on the door as I was having breakfast, and when Maria Elena offered him coffee, he joined me at the table and proceeded to help himself to the corn cakes on the platter. She and I had exchanged surprised glances, but when I shrugged, she placed a plate and silverware in front of him.

"I beg your pardon?" I said, frowning at him

"Woody," he said. "His death would make a great story."

"Story?"

"Here's a man most of us regarded as a good-humored buffoon."

"Well . . ."

"No, really, let me finish. Loud, cheery, always ready with a story. He had how many years in the military? There must have been a brain there somewhere. But he certainly was no intellectual. Retires to SMA, draws the women to him like flies. You wouldn't believe how many of these ladies he's squired around town. I never could see his appeal, but . . ." He trailed off.

"Maybe it had something to do with his cheerful disposition," I offered.

"Whatever. Here he is. He becomes the local mailman, in a sense, going on these forays to Laredo every month or so—I always wondered if he had a woman there too—and gets hijacked and murdered on the way home. It's perfect."

"I'm not sure what you mean by 'perfect,' " I said.

"Who would want to kill such a nice guy? That's the mystery."

"You think it was premeditated? You think whoever kidnapped Vaughan planned to kill Woody all along?"

"I'm not thinking of Vaughan."

My expression must have mirrored my disgust, because he hastened to say, "I mean he doesn't figure into the story. Olga will ransom him; everything will be fine. No, I'm thinking this is Woody's story."

I was thinking he was very quick to dismiss the danger to Vaughan.

"We can keep Vaughan in it if you want." He waved his hand as if this was of no consequence. "The story has great potential," he continued. "I hate to make use of a friend's misfortune, but when something falls into your lap you'd be a fool not to take advantage. We could really leverage this, you know, build up the mystery, put in some clues."

Thinking that I'd met many calculating people in my life and Roberto was right up there with the best of them, or rather the worst of them, I couldn't resist asking, "What did you have in mind?"

"You and I could team up to solve the murder and write it up for your next novel."

"You've been giving this quite some thought," I said.

"Well, sure. Haven't you? I'd like a co-credit, of course."

"Of course," I said, sure that the irony in my voice was lost on him.

"Did you take any notes yet?" he asked. "Because I have a lot of ideas." He reached into his breast pocket, drew out a small leather-bound book, and paged through it.

"At the moment I'm more interested in finding Vaughan Buckley alive and returning him home," I said. "I'm afraid you'll have to work on the murder mystery yourself."

"Let me tell you what I have so far," he said, oblivious to what I'd just said.

"Where's Dina this morning?" I asked, hoping to distract him.

"She went to Woody's apartment to help Philip pack his father's belongings."

"Is Philip ready to do that?" I asked. "He hasn't even made arrangements for the funeral yet."

"These young people have to be guided about what's right. He can't hang on to his father's things. It's morbid. Better to box them up right away. We can help him dispose of them."

"I don't know," I said, wondering how the Fishers got away with putting their noses into everyone's business. "I'd give him more time to mourn. Making decisions on what to keep and what to let go can be made later."

"No time like the present, to coin a phrase," he said. "You know if we keep Vaughan in it, Guy Kovach could be the one."

"The one what?"

"The one who set up the kidnapping."

Disappointed that my distraction had been short-lived, I resigned myself to entertaining Roberto's ideas. "Why would he do that?"

"For the money, of course."

"I could be mistaken," I said, "but Mr. Kovach appears to me to be quite a well-to-do man, in which case your motive is weak."

"See, that's what everyone thinks, but I'm telling you, the man's a fraud. Oh, he plays a good game, flashing all that jewelry on him and his wife. It's probably just paste, you know. Fake. It's easy to get that stuff copied."

He held up his cup and waved at Maria Elena, who brought a pot to the table and refilled his coffee. He scooped up a spoonful of sugar and lowered his voice confidentially. "The word going around is that he's broke."

"And?"

"And I can believe it," he said, clinking his spoon against the side of the mug as he quickly stirred his coffee. "Everything I ever bought on his say-so tanked."

"Who told you he's broke?"

"You mean names?"

"Yes."

He cleared his throat and hesitated before replying, "A couple of people hinted at it. I don't want to get them into trouble. It's just a rumor."

I had the feeling that I was sitting opposite the one who'd started the rumor. I didn't call him on it, but I did say, "Just because his stock recommendations didn't work out doesn't mean Mr. Kovach is broke. But even if he were, that fact alone doesn't suggest he's responsible for the kidnapping. And there's been a murder. Why would he kill Woody?"

"Woody was dispensable," Roberto said, regaining his confidence. "He doesn't have any money. He's not worth kidnapping. There's no one to pay ransom. Philip doesn't have two cents to rub together. He had to drop out of school."

"So you think Guy would simply kill Woody, a man who has been his friend, or at least someone with whom he's spent social time, because Woody wouldn't be worth robbing?" I gave him my sharpest look. "You'll have to come up with something better than that."

"I still think he did it."

"That may well be," I said, looking at him over the rim of my coffee cup, "but you'll need to prove it."

He consulted his notebook. "Well, Sarah Christopher's a possibility, too."

"You think she engineered the kidnapping and Woody's murder?"

"She and Woody were lovers and they broke up. Maybe she found out he was romancing another woman."

"And killed him out of jealousy?"

"It's not so far-fetched," he said, obviously annoyed with me. "You don't know the competition for dates in this town. There are a lot more women than men, at least in the expat community. The single women here are independent. They can be very aggressive, and they don't always confine their hunt to the bachelors, if you get my drift. Not that I'd ever tell Dina about it, but I've had my share of propositions."

An image of Sarah Christopher flirting with Vaughan came to mind.

"Maria Elena," I called.

"Yes, Señora?"

"Did Sarah Christopher ever come back yesterday afternoon?"

"No, Señora."

The artist had been so insistent that she would return, and when I indicated that it wouldn't be necessary, she'd chided me not to turn away help. I wondered what had kept her from coming back.

"Sarah's a good suspect, huh?"

"Hmm?" My mind had wandered and I wasn't paying attention to him.

"I said, Sarah makes a good suspect."

"Roberto, why don't you think about it a little more?" I said, wishing desperately that he'd leave. "We can talk again later."

"Gave you some good ideas, though, didn't I?" he said, pocketing his notebook with a smug smile. "I knew I would." He picked up his mug and slurped more coffee.

"It's very kind of you to keep me in mind," I said, folding my napkin. "Now, I have some things I need to do today, and the morning is getting away from me."

"Sure. Not a problem." He patted his breast pocket. "I'll type up my notes. There's a lot of good meat there."

The phone rang and I strained to hear Maria Elena's voice over Roberto's self-congratulations. She put the phone down and came to the table.

"Señora Buckley is on the phone. She wants to speak with you, Señora."

"Thank you, Maria Elena," I said, pushing back my chair.

Roberto put down his mug and politely got to his feet.

"Would you be good enough to escort Señor Fisher to the door?" I said to Maria Elena. "He was just leaving." I was darned if I was going to let Roberto eavesdrop on my conversation with Olga. "You'll excuse me, won't you?" I asked, shaking his hand. "I'm going to take this call upstairs. Please give my regards to your wife."

I hurried up to the media room and picked up the extension.

"Olga, I'm so glad to hear from you," I said.

"I'm sorry, Jessica. I know you tried to reach me yesterday," she said.

"It wasn't a problem. I know how busy you must be."

"It's true. I was. But on top of everything, the battery on my cell phone was dead, and I never realized it. I charged the phone all night and got your messages this morning. Have you heard anything more from the kidnappers?" she asked.

"Nothing so far," I said. "I checked the computer first thing when I woke up, and I'm signing on right now while we speak to see if there's any new e-mail. How did your meetings go?"

"The State Department was no help at all. They said they're cooperating with Mexican authorities but couldn't give me one concrete thing they're doing to help find Vaughan."

"They're probably relying on other agencies," I said.

"I had the feeling they were placating me. I don't know what I expected. They're certainly not going to send in troops. I understand that. But somehow I'd hoped our government would do more than simply go through the motions of professing sympathy when a U.S. citizen is taken captive in a foreign country. There was one funny thing, though."

"What was that?"

"I told the guy that Vaughan had been traveling with Woody. He said he knew Manheim from when they worked together in Mexico City. Can you believe it? Isn't it just like our government to assign someone to Mexico when they don't speak Spanish? Bureaucracy at work."

"What about Interpol?"

"They were more attentive. At least they asked for a photograph and wanted to know Vaughan's height, weight, blood type, and if he'd ever been fingerprinted."

"And has he?"

"Strangely enough, he has. Before he went into publishing he was teaching at a school in New York, and part of the background check included fingerprinting. Lord knows if they'll be able to find them, it was so long ago. And I didn't even like their asking for them. It says to me they want to be sure they can identify the body."

Olga was likely to be correct in her interpretation, but I said, as much for my comfort as hers, "You mustn't think that way. The police here are working on the case. We've got everyone on the alert. We're going to find him. And we're all going to celebrate his return."

"I'm praying every minute that you're right," she said. "Do you see anything on the computer?"

"No. I'm checking it now. There's nothing here."

"That's a bad sign, isn't it?"

"Not necessarily," I said. "They may be more aware of what's going on than we realize. They could be waiting for you to return with the money before they make their demands known."

"If they want that money, they'd better hand him over in good shape," she said. "I've been thinking about that, Jessica. Do you think I should offer a reward? I hate for these evil people to profit from their crime."

"Two people have already asked me if there's a reward for information," I said. "The more I think about it, the more I think it's not a good idea."

"Why not? Are you concerned that no one will come forward?"

"Quite the opposite," I said. "I think a lot of people would try to earn a reward if there was one."

"Then why not? I'd rather pay for information than give the kidnappers the money."

"There are two problems that I see," I said. "First, we might compromise the police investigation."

"In what way?"

"Many people in Mexico don't trust their police, sometimes for good reason. I happen to think Chief Rivera is honorable and responsible. I don't think he would act selfishly. But if people don't know that, they might hold back information, thinking they don't want the police to collect the reward instead of themselves."

"I hadn't thought of that."

"Another thing to consider is that the officers on the case might not work as hard if they think there's competition for the same information. That wouldn't help Vaughan. We want to keep the police on the alert. They're more likely to break the case than anyone else."

"I'm disappointed," she said. "I figured if we had a lot of people working on it, we'd find him sooner."

"We do have a lot of people working on it," I said, "but we need to be careful. We don't want to run the risk of spooking the kidnappers into taking a more drastic action, like abandoning Vaughan where he won't be found, or worse. No, I think we're better off leaving things as they are right now and holding off mentioning a reward."

"Anything you say, Jessica. I rely on your good judgment. All I want is my husband back safe." She paused a moment, then continued, her voice reflective. "It's peculiar being in the city without him, Jess. I couldn't stay in the apartment. It didn't feel right. I kept turning around to tell him something and realizing with a shock that he wasn't there. I checked into a hotel. I know it sounds foolish, but I kept thinking if I don't go places where we've been together, then it won't be as if he's not here."

"You're not being foolish," I said. "This is a terribly stressful time. You have to do whatever feels right for you. No one will fault you for that."

"I'll tell you one thing: I don't know what I would have done if you hadn't been there, Jessica. I can't think of a better person to leave in charge. I have confidence that if anyone can find Vaughan, it'll be you."

"The police are more likely to be his savior than I," I replied, "but if I can help them in any way, you know I will."

"I don't mean to burden you with my expectations. I'm just trying to say thank you and not doing a very good job of it. It must be nerve-racking to be checking the computer all day, waiting for them to send a message."

"No thanks are necessary," I said. "But I must tell you that I'm going to share that responsibility."

"Of course. Whatever you think best."

"I need to pay a visit to some people this afternoon. I'm going to have Maria Elena keep watch on the computer. She'll call me if she sees anything, and I'll call you if we hear from them."

"You may not be able to reach me," she said. "I almost forgot to tell you. I'm coming back today. I expect to finish up my financial affairs shortly, and I'll be on the next flight out."

"What time will you be here? Do you want me to call the Fishers or someone else to pick you up?" *So many people have said they stood ready to help,* I thought. *Here's a real opportunity to prove it.*

"No, don't bother about a ride. I'll make the arrangements. I don't know if I'll be able to get on a direct fight to León, but there are always lots of flights to Mexico City. I can't wait to get back. 'Bye, Jessica."

"Be careful, Olga," I said, but she'd already hung up. The flight from New York to Mexico City would get her here late afternoon at the earliest. Then there would be a flight to León, or if not, a four- or five-hour drive. Either way, there was a good chance she would be returning to San Miguel after dark. I just hoped she'd be safer on the road than I'd been.

Chapter Eighteen

After making sure Maria Elena was comfortable with the computer, I left the house and walked in the direction of El Jardin and police headquarters. As much as I'd been trying to put on a positive face for everyone, especially Olga, my spirits were not as buoyant as my outer appearance. I knew from past experience that the longer kidnappers held their victims, the less their chances of survival. Kidnappers are desperate people, and their patience runs out pretty quickly. If Vaughan's captors didn't feel they were close to succeeding in their quest for ransom money, they might decide to rid themselves of their victim and wait for a more promising opportunity.

I was consumed with that thought as I climbed the stairs to police headquarters and knocked on Chief Rivera's door. A gravelly voice shouted, *"¡Entre!"* I opened the door and stepped inside. Captain Gutierrez sat behind the chief's desk, his tooled cowboy boots propped up on its edge.

"What do you want?" he asked.

"I was hoping Chief Rivera was here," I answered.

"He is out of town till tomorrow. Police business. Come back then."

I ignored his brusque manner and sat down in a chair. "Since he's not here," I said, "perhaps you'll give me a few minutes of your time."

"I am busy."

"So am I," I said, not attempting to keep my pique from my voice. "I understand that Señor Manheim came here before he and Señor Buckley left on their trip."

His face screwed up in a quizzical expression as though not understanding my English. But I was sure he did, and I pressed on.

"I've been told that Señor Manheim made it a habit of telling the police whenever he was about to leave for Laredo to pick up mail there."

"It is not uncommon for the gringos to tell us when they are leaving," he said. He stretched his arms and yawned loudly.

"Did he speak with you personally?"

He pinched the bridge of his nose with two fingers and sighed.

I sat silently, awaiting his answer. From experience, I've learned that people often find silence disturbing and will rush to fill the void. This was a policeman, however, and I had to assume he knew all the tricks of interrogation. Nevertheless, I waited. I had time. He was the one who wanted me gone.

After a while he shrugged. "It is possible," he said. "I do not remember the conversations of every person who comes to the *delegación*. There are so many. We are busy all the time."

"It would seem to me that if people are in the habit of reporting their travels to the police, then they expect that information will be acted upon."

"I cannot be responsible for what people think."

"Are you saying that the police don't do anything? That it's a waste of time for people to report their travel plans to you? If that's the case, why don't you tell them not to bother?"

His nostrils flared at my remarks, and I knew he was annoyed, but he maintained his bored demeanor. "I don't say it's useless. Perhaps we will send a car to go down the street. That is all."

"And did Señor Manheim ask you to do that for him while he was gone?"

"Perhaps."

"What did he tell you?" I asked.

He gave me an exaggerated shrug. "He say he was going. That is all."

Pleased to see that he admitted having spoken with Woody, I pressed on. "Did he tell you that Señor Buckley was traveling with him?"

Another shrug.

"It's not so long ago. You must remember the conversation. Did he tell you Señor Buckley would be with him?" I repeated.

"Maybe, maybe not. I think maybe he did."

"When someone comes here to inform you that he is taking a trip and will be away for a while, does that information stay here?"

"No comprendo."

"Who else here, besides you, may have been aware of the trip?" I asked patiently. "Another officer? The chief?"

He dropped his feet from the edge of the desk to the floor. "I do not have to answer your questions, Señora. I am busy. *¿Comprende?* Very busy." He scowled and signaled with the back of his hand, dismissing me. "You may leave now."

I surmised from his response that he had, indeed, told others that Woody and Vaughan were leaving for Laredo and had undoubtedly included the date of their trip. If that information got into the wrong hands, either inside or outside the police station, it could account for the kidnappers' knowing where and when to mount their ambush.

I leaned back in the chair, consciously relaxing my shoulders, hoping my body language would convince him I wasn't leaving until he was more forthcoming. "I'll be happy to let you get back to your work," I said, "but before I go, I would appreciate it if you would be so kind as to give me your assessment of how your investigation into the kidnapping is going. Mrs. Buckley is returning today and will want to know. I don't think that's an unreasonable request."

His eyes turned calculating. "We have some good news," he said, cocking his head and raising one eyebrow.

I sat up straight. "You do?" Had he been toying with me

all this time? Did he know where Vaughan was? Were the investigators close to a rescue?

"Sí."

"What is it? What have you found?"

"It is what we have not found," he said. "The dogs, they did not find the body of your friend in the mountains."

My elation plummeted. He watched my face, and a small smile played on his lips. He was enjoying manipulating my emotions, and I was dismayed that I had allowed him the pleasure. "I didn't think they would," I persevered. "But what of your investigation? Do you have any leads on who the kidnappers might be?"

"We are working on it," he said, resuming his mask of indifference.

"And?"

"I do not discuss such things with civilians," he muttered.

Especially with female gringo civilians, I thought.

It was obvious that I wasn't about to learn anything else from this officer. I bade him good day and took my time gathering my purse and jacket before leaving. Once outside the office, however, I couldn't contain my frustration. I strode down the hall and descended the stairs to the street, rounding the corner so quickly I nearly bumped into a man in a blue shirt who was lounging against the building.

It was uncomfortably hot in the sun, and I considered crossing to El Jardin, where the abundant trees provided a cool awning. But I wanted to stop by Sarah Christopher's studio before finishing my intended rounds that day. Maria

Elena had written out instructions on how to get to the artist's lodgings. I found the street and walked downhill from El Jardin in the direction of the Parque Benito Juárez, where Olga and I had strolled together. Halfway between the two parks I saw Sarah standing outside a huge carved wooden door. Dressed in a loose tan smock with large patch pockets at the hips and streaks of blue paint down the front, she was speaking with a well-dressed Mexican man. They both turned to me as I approached.

"Hello, Jessica," she said.

"I hope I'm not intruding."

"Not at all," she replied. "This is Paulo Pedraga. He is an art dealer from Mexico City. Paulo, meet Jessica Fletcher. Jessica is an author."

"Sí?" he said, smiling broadly at me.

"She writes murder mysteries."

"It is my pleasure to meet you, Señora," he said, raising my hand to his lips.

I smiled back. "It's nice to meet you as well."

"Paulo is attempting to sell some of my paintings," she said.

"Yes, but she will not give me the best ones," he said, frowning at her.

"All my paintings are my best ones," she said archly.

"This may be. But like the characters in George Orwell's *Animal Farm,* some are more equal than others."

Sarah said something in Spanish. He nodded sharply and turned to me.

"Ladies, you must excuse me," he said. "I have several

stops to make in San Miguel. A city full of artists. What could be better for a dealer than that?"

Sarah replied tartly in Spanish. He laughed and promised that he would return later that day.

"Come on in," she said, wiping perspiration from her brow with a handkerchief. "I made some fresh iced tea. It's too hot to stand outside in the sun."

There was something different about her today, and I couldn't quite put my finger on it. She was subdued, a weary expression on her face. It made her appear older than I had originally perceived her to be.

We crossed a narrow courtyard and entered her house. Inside, it was considerably cooler than on the street, the building's stone structure providing natural air-conditioning. Sarah's studio was on the main floor in what would ordinarily have been the living room. It was a large space completely given over to her work, with tall windows open to the courtyard on one side and to an alley on the other.

She was obviously hard at work. Two wooden easels held paintings, each with a piece of wrinkled canvas thrown over it to hide the unfinished composition from prying eyes. The easels stood on either end of a rough planked table, on which were cans of turpentine, linseed oil, and a jug of what appeared to be dirty water. Used coffee cans, mayonnaise jars, and assorted other kitchen containers held brushes, palette knives, and half-squeezed tubes of paint. A vase of flowers stood next to a plate with leftovers from a recent meal, and a pile of soiled rags sat on a laptop computer. She had one tall stool, which must have served both the easels, and a smaller table strewn with an array of bottles, pens, paints, and thin brushes, as well as a carton containing paper with a pile of miscellaneous items dumped on top—keys, wadded tissues, a wallet, a bracelet, coins—as if she'd emptied her pockets into the box. Stacks of paintings, some clearly unfinished, leaned against the walls. Pen-and-ink drawings rendered in blue and red were hanging at angles, tacked up on a long wall.

An arched opening at one end of the room led to the kitchen and dining room, both a riot of colorful tiles, fabrics, and accessories. A radio, set to loud, played Latin music. Sarah switched it off on her way into the kitchen.

I glanced around for a chair. Apart from the stool, the only place to sit was a battered upholstered sofa, the seat cushions concave with age and covered with serapes, their different patterns both clashing and blending with each other and with the large and small pillows casually thrown against the back. I decided not to chance it, having too often struggled to rise from an overly soft seat or one where the springs were long gone. I remained standing and inspected the work on the walls.

When she returned from her kitchen with two tall glasses of iced tea garnished with mint leaves, I said, indicating the paintings, "It looks like you're in a particularly productive mode, Sarah."

"I'm trying to gather enough work for a show, but it's tricky," she said. "My productivity ebbs and flows, like the tides and phases of the moon. When I get into a particularly industrious mood, I try to take advantage of it, knowing it will fade and I won't produce anything worthwhile." She set the tea down on her worktable, pushing the plate out of the way, and fetched a chair from the dining room for me. "For some reason, tragedy always spurs me on," she said, leaning on the high back of the chair. "Maybe I use my work as an escape." She dropped her chin and shook her head. "I still can't believe it," she said.

I knew instantly what she was referring to. "Yes, it is shocking."

"No one told me that Woody had been killed," she said, her voice hard, her eyes boring into mine. "I had to hear it on the radio."

"You didn't know?"

"No. I only knew he and Vaughan had been kidnapped."

"I'm so sorry you weren't informed right away, Sarah. I assumed someone would tell you."

"It doesn't matter. What's done is done." She slapped her hand on the top of the chair. "Damn!" she said, pacing to the window. "He must have resisted, tried to fight them off. Mr. Macho Man, Woody was, full of bravado, self-professed soldier of fortune. Damn!"

"I know you were particularly close to him," I offered.

She swung back to glare at me. "Close? Like in lovers?"

"I had the impression that you and he might have had a romantic relationship, but maybe I was wrong."

"You're right, Jessica. You were wrong. Woody was a friend, that's all. He might have wanted more at one time and tried to initiate it, but I discouraged him. He was too old for me, not so much in age as in attitude. Anyway, I like younger men. I know I hurt him by feeling that way, but he had many women to choose from. He didn't suffer long."

"But you remained good friends," I said.

She shrugged. "Sure. Why not? He was a good guy. His heart was in the right place, unlike most of the expats around here. They have no appreciation for the people whose country they're happy to inhabit. All they care is that nothing gets in the way of their privileged lives now and then. They should try living for a day like the majority of poor Mexicans," she snorted, "like the people who work for them. If they did, they might see things differently."

She delivered her expression of empathy with conviction. I knew only a little of the plight of poor Mexicans, my knowledge confined to what I'd read about uprisings that had taken place over the years and the government's attempts to quell them. Rebelling against in-place governments by impoverished citizens certainly wasn't unique to Mexico. It happened in myriad countries around the world, cries for justice and equality too often deteriorating into outright revolution, bloodshed, and thousands of shattered lives.

"You're very passionate about this subject," I said.

"You can't live here, Jessica, and not be," she said in a tone leaving no room for debate. "At least I can't."

"I'm not surprised, given the subjects of your paintings, like the one you sold to Olga and Vaughan."

Her expression registered discomfort for a moment; then her face cleared. "Don't you want your tea?" she asked, pushing the chair in my direction with one hand and handing me the glass with the other.

I took the tea, turned the chair around to face her, and sat quietly, sipping. Sarah perched on the stool, her glass of tea untasted in her hand.

"How did you happen to come to San Miguel?" I asked. "You're too young to be retired and trying to stretch a pension like a lot of the other Americans. Was it the art community that drew you?"

"I used to live in Texas. I moved to San Miguel fifteen years ago because of a man I'd fallen in love with." She held the cold glass up to her face, rolling it against her cheek. Her eyes closed, seeing visions from her past, not the guest sitting in front of her. I watched the emotions flit across her face, pleasure morphing into distress. Abruptly, she focused on her hand, gulped half the tea, and set the glass down heavily on the table. "He was Mexican, handsome, bright, and committed to his cause," she said, turning to face me.

"Which was?"

"Freedom, of course," she replied. "What other cause is there? He fought the oppression of the people by the government. He was full of fire and zeal, and eventually I was, too, because of him."

"What happened to him?" I asked, not sure I should.

"He was murdered, too."

"How dreadful."

"He led a demonstration in a small village south of here. It wasn't much of a rebellion. Workers at a factory went on strike to protest their pitiful wages and lack of benefits. The government sent troops to quell what they considered a dangerous riot." She guffawed. "Dangerous riot, indeed. He stood at the head of the strikers and shouted the demands they were making. Soldiers opened fire and gunned him, and some of the strikers, down in front of me."

"You were there?"

She nodded. "I had his body brought back here to San Miguel and arranged for his burial."

"I'm so sorry," I said. "It must have been a traumatic time."

She gave me a wry smile. "San Miguel is becoming a city of losses for me. But you didn't come here to discuss my love life. Or did you?"

"No, of course not," I said. "You had indicated you were coming back to the house yesterday, and you didn't return. I just wanted to make sure you were all right."

"That's very kind of you," she said in a tone that hinted that she thought I wasn't being truthful.

"Who have you spoken to about Woody's death?" I asked.

"I don't recall," she said, stroking the brushes in one of the paint cans. "It was all over town shortly after I left the Buckleys' house—on the radio, on television." She sighed and gazed up at me. "How is the tea?"

"Terrific. I pride myself on the iced tea I make back home in Maine, but yours is delicious, too. The mint leaves give it a wonderful flavor."

She took a brush from the can, swirled it around in the dirty water, and rubbed it with a corner of the paint-stained rag. "Everyone has a skill they can call their own," she said.

I couldn't tell if she was being snide. "I know I'm intruding on your work, Sarah. I have the same problem you do when I'm writing a book. Some days the words just flow, and I try to turn out as many pages as possible. Other days—"

"Art and the artist," she said, brightening. "The eternal question: Where does creativity come from, and how do you keep it flowing year after year? What's your answer?"

"I wish I had one," I said, sipping my tea.

The telephone rang. She excused herself and left the room.

In her absence, I got up from my chair and went to where her new works were displayed on the wall. The line drawings and washes were very different from the art hanging in Vaughan and Olga's home, more impressionistic than those gracing my friends' living room wall and more sophisticated than the younger work in their dining room and hall. She was working in a different medium, using watercolors and inks instead of the oils I was used to seeing. Was she experimenting with something new, or making an effort to paint in a style more appealing to prospective buyers? As I examined her work, my eyes strayed to the table with the ink bottles and boxes of pens. What I had earlier taken to be a bracelet was, on second glance, not a piece of women's jewelry at all. It was a man's watch with a woven leather band, and if I wasn't mistaken, it was the watch that Woody's son, Philip, claimed to have misplaced.

Interesting, I thought. Had he come to the studio to tell Sarah of his father's murder? For consoling? That seemed a safe assumption. Why Sarah, I wondered, and not another of his father's friends? It might not mean anything. Still, a man didn't usually remove his watch, unless . . . Were Sarah and Philip engaged in an affair? I judged her to be in her early forties; Philip was considerably younger, barely out of his teens. But she said she liked younger men. And men of any age would be drawn to her dark beauty and intensity, her talent and passion. What ran through my mind at that moment was that if that scenario were true—that Woody's young son was romantically involved with a woman his father had coveted—it could spawn some pretty strong feelings between father and son.

I returned my attention to the art on the easels. Lifting a corner of the covering, I studied what she'd hidden from view. This was the kind of oil painting I'd begun to associate with her, dark and violent. But I thought I remembered Olga saying those were early works. Why would she be working on a painting she had finished years ago? I leaned close to see the detail in the scene. It was a montage of Mexican peasants. Some held rifles above their heads, or pitchforks and other farm tools. Their faces were set in anger. But not all of them. Sarah had started to paint out the faces of two figures. One was completely obscured, but the features of the other were still visible through the thin layer she'd brushed over them. He stood in the center of the group, and if I wasn't mistaken, the face belonged to Woody Manheim.

Sarah's sudden reappearance in the room startled me, and I bumped against the table holding the inks and watercolors, causing the liquids to slosh around in their containers.

"Don't get that ink on you," she said. "It's permanent." She held out her smock to show me the stains.

"An occupational hazard," I said.

"Yes." She noticed the watch on the table and scooped it up, dropping it into a pocket.

"Thanks for letting me interrupt your creative efforts today, Sarah," I said.

"I needed the break," she said.

She walked me to the street.

"Mind a word of advice?," she said.

"I'd welcome it."

"Don't hold out too much hope for Vaughan."

"Oh?"

"I'll be really surprised if he doesn't suffer the same fate as Woody."

"Why would you say that?"

"It's a violent world."

"Well," I said, taken aback, "I certainly hope you're wrong."

Chapter Nineteen

I stepped outside Sarah's carved door and came face-to-face with Captain Gutierrez.

"What are you doing here?" he demanded.

"I came to visit Sarah Christopher," I said. "I assume you're here for the same reason. Am I right?"

"I do not have to tell you my business," he said, brushing past me and slamming the door behind him.

I sighed. The sky had turned dark gray, reflecting my mood and heralding the arrival of rain sooner or later. Low rumbles from a distance, barking dogs, and the pealing of church bells, a common sound in San Miguel de Allende, assaulted my ears. The Buckleys' house was not too far from here, but in which direction? I started walking uphill, changed my mind and turned back toward the Parque Benito Juárez. Down the cobblestone street, a man in a blue shirt pulled his hat lower on his face and slipped into an open doorway. Farther away, I could make out the beginnings of a pageant of some sort. Mounted horsemen carrying flags and wearing sombreros edged in dark colors were lined up in formation, the bobbing noses of their steeds pointed in my direction. I decided it would be easier to get my bearings if I returned to my El Jardin starting point and found my way back to Olga's from there.

The sound of wood slapping against something solid above me caused me to look up. A woman had flung open the shutters on her window and now leaned out. I suppose my face reflected my question about what was occurring. She grinned down at me. "Fiesta!" she called out. "Fiesta!"

The horsemen were moving closer, the hooves of their mounts audible on the cobblestones, and the rumbles I'd heard clarified into the beating of drums, the sounds competing with the barks and howls of the dogs in the courtyards of homes up and down the street. I watched the parade draw near and saw the man in the blue shirt emerge from the doorway. Other doors opened and children and their parents spilled into the street, the little ones hopping and dancing as the procession made its way uphill. They raced toward me, laughing, their parents calling out to caution them. The man remained where he was. He wouldn't have captured my attention except that I was sure I'd seen him before, when I went to police headquarters that morning. Just a coincidence, I told myself as I turned uphill toward El Jardin, scarcely a block ahead of the parade.

When I reached the park's perimeter, I paused and waited for the horsemen to pass by me into the square. I craned my neck to see where I'd come from, checking for my tracker. *You're being foolish,* I told myself. *If he's there, he's just coming to watch the fiesta.* Even so, I considered approaching him should he show up again, but my view was suddenly cut off by a line of women in black dresses with purple stoles, two of whom held aloft a picture of a saint, presumably the one in whose honor the festival was being held. In the midst of them was a wooden cart made to resemble a white coffin with black outlines drawn on it. Standing in the coffin replica were children dressed in white with colorful bands across their chests, like beauty pageant contestants but with a more serious purpose.

Concha dancers, bare-chested but for intricately detailed breastplates, followed next. I wondered how they could keep their balance in the huge feathered headdresses shaped like giant disks, which were easily more than half the height of their bodies. But they not only kept their balance, they danced to the beat of the drums, their steps at first measured, then as the tempo increased, more frenzied. The people in the park deserted their benches and gathered for a closer look at the dancers. I was swept along with the crowd as they moved toward the entrance to La Parroquia, the huge Gothic church that towered over the square.

Bringing up the rear of the procession were two mariachi bands, one female and one male. The women wore long sky blue skirts with matching bolero jackets on which white flowers were embroidered, while the men were in tight black suits with gold and silver fringe down the sides of their pants and along the sleeves of their jackets, their hats large and colorfully fringed. Each band played its own music, the sounds of their trumpets, guitars, bass guitars, and violins adding to the general cacophony, the notes blending and competing as the musicians moved into the street in front of the church, the whole accompanied by the pealing from La Parroquia's spires, which drowned out all other sounds every few seconds as the heavy bells reached the zenith of their arc and the clappers pounded out their heavy knells.

Around me were Mexican men in historical costumes consisting of white pajamas and sandals, similar to figures commonly seen in the paintings of Diego Rivera, and everywhere was the sound of drums whose incessant beating was louder than the thunder I thought I'd heard.

The festivities filled El Jardin, where vendors, who sold their wares daily in the park, had decorated their carts with Mexican flags and red, white, and green bunting. The park was packed with people; locals and tourists alike mixed with the costumed revelers, the atmosphere bursting with celebration and joy. I flinched as the sound of fireworks burst overhead. *You're jumpy today, Jessica,* I told myself.

I realized I hadn't eaten since breakfast, and cast about for a vendor with something that appealed. Olga had said that the ice cream offered in the park was excellent, and safe to eat. A cool ice cream sounded appealing, and I sought out a cart, bought a large cone from the old fellow manning it, and found a vacant spot on a bench beneath the canopy of a large tree. I took a lick and looked around. The man I'd seen twice before was there again, leaning against a tree a few feet away.

Who are you? I wondered.

Are you following me?

If you are, why are you doing it?

I was about to get up and ask him when my vision was blocked by the sudden arrival of a young man with a large box suspended from a multicolored cord around his neck. Two small wire cages were side by side, close to his body. In each of the cages was a live canary. In front of the cages were two sections of the box, recessed to allow the top of their contents to be even with the surface of the box. Hundreds of tiny slips of paper were in the sunken sections, yellow on one side, pink on the other.

"Señora," the young man said with a wide smile, "you speak English, yes?"

"Yes," I said, trying to peer around him to see whether the man was still by the tree.

"Your fortune," said the young man in good English. "Pauchito and Estelita will perform for the lovely lady and tell her what her future will be."

"Pauchito and—? Oh, those are the names of the birds?"

"Sí, Señora. They are very wise birds. You will be pleased with what they tell you."

"I don't think so," I said. "I really don't—"

He leaned closer to me. "It is important that you do," he said. "What they tell you is very important."

"It is? All right. How much will it cost?"

"Whatever you wish to give me, Señora. I know you will be generous."

"Go ahead," I said. "I'm ready to hear my fortune."

He opened the door to one of the cages and the bird hopped out onto the slips of paper. "Pauchito will entertain you first," he said.

I watched as the tiny bird went through an impressive array of tricks, including picking up a tiny hat in its beak, tossing it into the air, ducking under it so it landed on its head, and then shaking it off. It also rang a small bell with its beak on command, stopped when told to by its owner, and rang it again upon instruction.

"That's wonderful," I said, meaning it. "I never realized birds could be trained this way."

"Only these birds, Señora. Now, your fortune." He said to the bird, "Choose carefully, Pauchito. It is very important for the señora that you choose carefully."

The bird walked in circles over the slips of paper. It stopped on top of the pink section, dipped its beak into the papers, and withdrew one.

"Your hand, Señora," the man said.

I extended my right hand, palm up, and Pauchito dropped the paper into it.

"*Gracias,*" I said. "Thank you."

"*De nada,* Señora. It is my pleasure and my little friends' pleasure, too."

I pulled money from my purse and handed it to him.

"You are too generous, Señora. Thank you. Thank you."

I watched him walk away and couldn't help but smile. It was a charming interlude, one whose memory I would hold for a long time. I looked at the small slip of pink paper, which I'd crumpled into a ball, and was about to drop it into a trash receptacle next to the bench when I remembered what he'd said—that the fortune it contained was important. It was more than just a sales pitch. He'd meant it.

My eyes sought the man in the blue shirt, who I was certain had been following me, but he was nowhere to be seen. I opened the paper, pulled reading glasses from my purse, and squinted to read the tiny type.

"Oh, my," I said as what was written sank in. "Oh, my."

Chapter Twenty

"It's not much, I know," Dina said, patting the box of Mexican wedding cookies she'd set on the table, "but I made them myself. I like a sweet when I'm upset, so I thought you would, too."

"That was very considerate of you," I said, regretting that the chop Maria Elena had cooked for my dinner was cooling on the plate and wondering how it was that one of the Fishers seemed always to show up when a meal was being served. Dina had arrived and taken the chair opposite mine at the table under the colonnade soon after I'd started eating. I'd put down my fork and knife, of course, not wanting to be rude. But now my food was cold and she showed no signs of leaving. Reluctantly, I asked the question I knew she was waiting for. "Would you like something to eat?"

"Sure. Do you have enough? I don't want to impose."

Maria Elena set another place at the table and put a

plateful of food in front of our guest. I hoped she wasn't serving Dina the portion she had intended for herself.

Dina dug into the food, wiped her mouth with a napkin, and looked around.

"Anything wrong?" I asked.

"I need something to drink."

"What would you like?"

"A margarita would be nice."

"I don't know how to make one, but Maria Elena may."

"Oh, you don't have to bother her," she said, standing. "I'm a whiz at margaritas. I'll make it myself."

She entered the kitchen and made straight for the cabinet in which Vaughan kept his liquor bottles and barware. I heard the refrigerator door being opened and shut. Moments later she was back at the table with two cocktail glasses filled to the brim with a light green concoction.

"I'm afraid I forgot to tell you that I didn't want one for myself," I said. "I'm sorry you went to the trouble."

"Don't be ridiculous," she said cheerfully, setting a glass down in front of me. "I'd never drink alone. Besides, the coolness of the margarita is a great counterpoint to the spicy food. Every good chef will tell you that." She took her seat, shook out her napkin, draped it across her lap, and lifted her glass. "*Salud*," she said, clinking her glass against mine.

I took a sip of the drink and put it down. It was very good, but I wanted to keep a clear head for my evening appointment. Idly, I speculated on the timing of Dina's visit. Why had she shown up now? What did she want—other than food?

"Have you heard from Olga?" she asked, tucking into her meal again.

"Yes, I have. She's on her way back here."

"That's terrific," she said. "Did she get the money?"

There was not the slightest chance I was going to discuss the Buckleys' finances with her. "I didn't ask," I said truthfully.

"I'm sure she did. They must be swimming in it if she could put a million together so fast, don't you think?"

My mother taught me as a little girl that when someone asks a rude question, don't answer. Simply pose a different question of your own. Her advice has come in handy many times, and I employed it again. "Where is Roberto this evening?" I asked.

"He's writing. He said you and he are going to collaborate on a book, and he's been glued to the computer all day."

I wasn't about to tell her that I hadn't agreed to her husband's suggestion, nor that it was never likely to happen. Instead I said, "My publisher may have something to say about that. I'm under contract, after all."

Dina was ready with an answer. "Since your publisher could be a victim of his captors, that may all be moot."

She was the second person that day to assume the kidnappers would kill Vaughan, and like Sarah, she seemed unfazed by the prospect. While I had to acknowledge that it was not out of the realm of possibility, I was far from accepting their predictions. I put down my knife and fork, my appetite completely gone. "I'm hopeful Vaughan will be returned unharmed," I said, "but in any case, the contract is with his firm and would still be binding."

"You have to be realistic, Jessica. After all, this is Mexico. We hear about these kinds of things all the time, though granted, not in SMA. Still, people are killed every day all over the country." She lowered her voice and shot a glance toward the kitchen. "You can't really trust these people, you know."

"No, I don't know. Everyone I've met has been trust-worthy," I said, deliberately excluding the *bandido* who'd waylaid me on my way to San Miguel.

"Well, be that as it may, it's not always the case." She took a piece of a roll, sopped up the gravy on her plate, chewed thoughtfully, and sipped her drink, finishing it quickly. "I understand you were at Woody's the other night," she said. "How is Philip doing?"

Her question surprised me. "Weren't you there this morning helping him pack?" I asked. "That's what Roberto said. In that case, you would know better than I."

"I went there, but he wasn't home. If you're not going to finish that," she said, indicating my drink, "may I?"

"Go ahead," I said, handing her my glass.

She smiled. "Yum. Anyway, I called Philip yesterday to tell him what time I'd be there, but the place was locked when I arrived."

"Maybe he's not ready to dispose of his father's belong-ings," I said, thinking that it may have been the first time Philip had ever locked his front door. "After all, the funeral hasn't even taken place yet."

She shrugged. "Maybe. What did you think of his apartment?"

"Woody's?"

"Yes."

"I imagine it served him and Philip well."

"Did you find anything of interest?"

"I wasn't looking for anything of interest," I replied. "I was merely delivering food Maria Elena had prepared."

"C'mon, Jessica. Everyone knows you're investigating the murder. It's the buzz all over town. I'm surprised they haven't put it in the paper yet."

"You can't believe everything you hear, Dina."

"Well, I can certainly believe that."

Maria Elena came to the table and eyed my plate, which was mostly untouched. "Would you like something else, Señora?"

"Not for me, thank you," I said. "Dina?"

"No. I've gotta go," she said, finishing my drink. "Thanks anyway. Dinner was good."

Maria Elena cleared away the dishes and the box of cookies after Dina left, and I sat thinking about this strange visit. It would appear that she was probing to find out something, but what? Was she simply a neighborhood gossip on the hunt for tidbits she could pass along? I knew people like that back home. They enjoyed knowing what others did not, and felt superior when they could contribute to the community grapevine or, as was often the case, the rumor mill. But this was not a practice I cared to participate in. Nor was I especially pleased to learn that the expatriate community in San Miguel was convinced I was investigating Woody's murder. Of course, Dina could be exaggerating, a trait not uncommon among heavy drinkers, which she seemed to be. Either way, and regardless of public or private opinion, my priority was clear. Helping to free Vaughan was much more important to me, especially now that people were automatically counting him out.

"The wedding cookies are very—how do you say it?—typical of my country," Maria Elena said, setting a small dish in front of me on which she had placed three of the little pastry balls dredged in powdered sugar. "Is that correct?"

"I think the word you're looking for is 'authentic.' "

"Sí! They are very authentic. But it is not the proper occasion."

I picked up a cookie and leaned forward to taste it, trying to keep from spattering powdered sugar on my blouse.

"Would you like some coffee?" she asked.

"I think under the circumstances it would be a good idea," I said. "Will you join me? We need to talk."

Maria Elena returned from the kitchen with two cups of coffee. She placed one in front of me and studied my face. "Señora, you cannot go alone," she said, sitting down. "I will go with you."

"The instructions were very specific that I come by myself."

I had shared with Maria Elena the "fortune" that the little canary had picked out for me. It was a message telling me to be at a certain place at ten o'clock that evening and not to call the police. Olga wasn't back with the money yet, and I had no idea what time she would arrive, but I feared that if I failed to keep the assignation, Vaughan's life might be forfeited.

Maria Elena chewed her cheek, her eyes worried. "I am afraid, Señora. Hector told me Father Alfredo said they must be desperate men to do what they did. These men, they could be planning to kidnap you, too, and hold you for ransom."

"I suppose that's a possibility," I allowed, "but you said La Filomela is a cantina."

"Sí. It is very popular, always crowded. Many tourists go there."

"I doubt they'd be planning to abduct me from a public place."

"If they will take you away, no one will see that you are missing. This place, it is *too* busy."

"I imagine they chose the cantina for that precise reason—because no one will notice them coming or going. And if tourists go there, the presence of an American woman won't be unusual. No one will find it strange that I'm there."

"What will I say to Señora Buckley if you are taken? She will think that I did not look out for you. Maybe she will think that I am involved, that I am responsible."

"She will think no such thing," I said. "She trusts you, and so do I. As for tonight's meeting, it's a chance I have to take. I don't believe they have another kidnapping in mind."

"How can you know? This is so terrible." She wrung her hands.

"Well, I can't be absolutely positive, but a man followed me for much of today, and at no time did he attempt to harm or capture me."

She drew in a sharp breath. "You were followed?"

"I'm fairly certain I was."

She gripped the edge of the table. "I will call my brother now. He will come with you to protect you."

I put my hand on her arm. "You're very kind, and please don't think I'm not grateful for your concern," I said, "but calling Hector is not a good idea. For all we know, the kidnappers may have someone watching the house at this very moment or eavesdropping on the telephone line. Whoever sent me this message said to come alone. If he sees me with your brother, he may think I'm trying to trap him and he might not approach me. If so, we'll have lost an opportunity to save Vaughan."

"Then I can take a message to the police for you. The kidnappers, they will not think to follow me. The police can send someone to stand at the bar or sit at a table. I saw that on television once. They pretend to be customers. The kidnappers, they will never know. You could suggest it."

"I could," I said, "but Chief Rivera is out of town, and I'm not confident his deputy would even listen to me. Besides, if he did, I can't be sure that he wouldn't grab the first opportunity to arrest someone. Any action by the police could worsen the danger for Vaughan. No, I can't risk his life to safeguard mine."

"But what will I tell the señora when she comes home?"

"You can tell her I've gone out to look for Vaughan."

She shook her head sadly. "I will pray for your safety."

"Thank you, Maria Elena. I need all the help I can get."

Chapter Twenty-one

La Filomela, the Nightingale, was on a small street on the other side of town, a considerable distance from the Buckleys' home. There was nothing in its dark interior to explain its popularity. The décor was nondescript, the lighting dim, the air smoky. Long wooden tables, their edges polished by the elbows and forearms of countless customers, filled the room. A continuous bench ran along the wall opposite the long bar. Patrons who wanted to sit were forced to share the company of whoever occupied a table first, squeezing onto the bench or pulling up a chair wherever there was space to place a glass. The only other choice was to drink standing up, since the bar had no stools. The compulsory mingling meant a stranger might easily be made to feel at home, or just as easily be made acutely aware of her solitude in the heart of a crowd.

How are they ever going to find me in this crush? I thought. I pushed my way past a group of students who were jockeying for the attention of the bartenders, and looked for a place to sit. The members of a mariachi band were unpacking their instruments in the corner away from the door, and I was fortunate to find space at the end of a table near them when a couple got up to leave.

The chair next to mine was empty, and I rested my jacket on it so that people would think I had someone with me and look elsewhere for a seat. The other people at the table were young, three couples in their twenties, regaling each other with stories that evidently were hilarious, judging from their loud laughter. Amid their merriment, my mind drifted to Vaughan. Was he all right? Was he sick with worry that his life was over, that he would be killed? Was he pleading for his life like the terrified prisoners in Iraq who had been paraded on international television before their cruel captors beheaded them? An involuntary shiver went through me. Where could they be keeping him? Was he tied up in a cellar somewhere? Were they giving him food and water? The editor of *Noticias* had said San Miguel was a small town that couldn't keep a secret. Why had nothing surfaced about Vaughan so far? Was he being held outside San Miguel? I would have to visit the newspaper office again to see if the editor had learned anything. And why was Chief Rivera off somewhere when Vaughan was still missing? This was his big case. *Why is he not combing the streets and neighborhoods instead of leaving that oaf Gutierrez in charge?*

The musicians began to tune up. The first notes of the guitar were plucked, then joined by a chorus from the trumpets and a sharp downbeat from the fiddle. I always find it interesting that most people reserve the word *violin* for the instrument used when classical music is being played, but call it *fiddle* when the music is that of country people. Truth be told, the sound of a mariachi fiddle is a far cry from the violin concertos of Beethoven and Brahms, but it does have a spirited kinship with American country-and-western music and with Louisiana's Cajun and zydeco bands, where the "fiddle" personality is more fitting.

I twisted around in my chair to watch the musicians, grateful for the distraction. If the note from the canary proved to be a hoax—if no one showed up and I sat in the bar for hours—at least the music would be compensation for the effort. It was hard to stay miserable in the face of mariachi music, with its bracing tempo and exhilarating feel. I only wished Vaughan and Olga were there to enjoy it with me.

The members of the band were not attired in the traditional mariachi costume, or *traje de charro*. Instead of the short jacket and tight pants, trimmed with embroidery or silver buttons, and the large formal sombrero, they were bareheaded and wore blue jeans and plaid shirts. They looked as if they'd just gotten off work and decided on the spur of the moment to get together to play music and celebrate. In fact, the whole cantina was in a celebratory mood—and I was its lone false note. The band struck up a new song and began walking down the line of tables playing requests, the crowds parting as they approached, everyone eager to hear them.

A buxom waitress in a black miniskirt and a hot-pink peasant blouse exposing both her shoulders came to the table. She held a small tray on which was an array of bottles. "*Cerveza, Señora?*" she shouted over the music.

"I beg your pardon."

"Beer. Corona, Sol, Dos Equis, Casta, Pacífico, Simpatico, Brise, Negra Modelo, Tequiza, Indio," she said, rattling off the brands available.

"What would you suggest?" I asked, wondering if the kidnappers were even now watching my every move.

"Try the Casta," a masculine voice next to me suggested. "It's a nice ale. You'll like it." He said something to the waitress, who deposited a bottle and a napkin in front of me.

"*Limón?*" she asked.

"She wants to know if you want lime. Say yes."

"Sí," I said.

The waitress pushed a wedge of lime into the open neck of the bottle.

My advisor tossed a bill on her tray, and she departed.

"You don't have to pay for my beer," I said, turning to see who my benefactor was and opening my bag to find my wallet.

"Please put away your money. It's my pleasure to welcome you to San Miguel," said the man who had just taken the seat next to mine. "Is this your jacket? I almost sat on it." He was a wiry man in his forties, his thick black hair slicked back from his forehead, his handsome features marred by deep acne scars on his cheeks. Despite his thin physique, his arms were sinewy, raised veins visible against his dusky skin, the tips of his fingers calloused but the nails clean. I speculated that he worked with his hands, but in what capacity I wasn't sure. The educated tones of his lightly accented English indicated that he was something other than a laborer.

I took the jacket and laid it across my lap, wondering if this was the person I'd been saving the seat for. "The least I can do is thank you and introduce myself," I said. "I'm Jessica Fletcher, visiting here from the States."

"I know who you are," he said. "You can call me Alfredo. I am here on behalf of a friend of yours, or more accurately one who would be a friend."

"And who is that?" I asked.

"His name doesn't matter. You have met him before, when you first came to San Miguel."

"And why isn't he here himself?"

"He is not well. And also, he does not speak English. But this man, who would be your friend, has sent me with a gift. He said you will know who he is when I give it to you." He gently took my hand, reached into his pocket, pulled out a crumpled piece of paper tied with string, and dropped it in my palm.

"What is this?"

"Open it and you will see," he said. "You were a heroine to him recently. My friend, he gives you this gift."

I untied the string and carefully folded back the paper. What little light there was in the cantina reflected off the gold circle set with tiny rubies. "Oh, my," I said, my eyes welling up. It was the ring my late husband, Frank, had given me when we were courting, the ring I'd been heart-broken to lose, the ring that had been stolen by the *bandido*.

"Thank you," I whispered, putting on the ring, rejoicing in its familiar touch, a memento of the love with which it had originally been presented. So foolish we humans are to attach importance to material possessions. This ring was not worth risking my life or that of my young driver, Juanito. I had recognized that immediately. Yet this little loop of gold was a link to my past, a keepsake of our years together, Frank's and mine, and I treasured it.

"You saved his child from being killed by the big bus," Alfredo said. "He is very grateful. He said he cannot return the other items you kindly gave him. They were bartered for food for his family. He is very sorry for that."

I swallowed hard and turned to Alfredo. "He told you about the robbery?"

"It has been weighing on his mind. What is it they say? 'Confession is good for the soul.' He needed to make amends."

"I understand," I said. "Please thank him for me. And tell him I forgive him."

"He will be most relieved to learn how kind the señora is. However, he sent another message to you, and perhaps you will not be so pleased with this one."

I braced myself. "Is it about Vaughan? Vaughan Buckley?"

"If that is the name of your friend who was taken away. Yes, it is about him."

"He's not—" I couldn't bring myself to voice my fears.

"Dead? No, no. I assure you, he is still among the living."

A long breath whooshed out of me. "Thank goodness for that. Is he uninjured? Do you know who's holding him or where he is? The police are looking everywhere. It's urgent that you tell me what you know." Waves of questions swamped my mind. I was close to finding Vaughan now. Here was our first break, someone who knew who the kidnappers were, perhaps where they held Vaughan.

"Patience, patience, Señora. I am only the messenger, not a part of the plot, nor one of the hostage takers. I only know what I am told and what I have been told to tell you."

"Your friend is the balloon vendor. Am I correct?"

"He thought you recognized him. He is afraid to come forward. There is no one else to take care of his children."

"And is he part of the plot, one of the hostage takers? I can forgive him for theft, but I cannot conceive that he would dare to think that returning my ring would make up for killing one man and kidnapping another, putting their families through such anguish."

"He has killed no one," Alfredo said. "He was not even there."

"Then I don't understand. How does he know that Vaughan is all right?"

"He was not at the scene, the night of the kidnapping, but he blames himself all the same. You see, our friend, he was supposed to be there that night. A man they call El Grande had recruited him, had promised him money, but our friend, he was too sick to go. The others, they hired another at the last moment, and it was he . . ." He hesitated, unsure of how to phrase the information. "He was young and hotheaded. And the man who was killed, he behaved in a manner that was threatening. No one was supposed to be hurt. It was all a misunderstanding."

"A misunderstanding! Now listen to me," I said. "Taking a man's life is not simply a misunderstanding. Whoever this person was, he shot Woody and left him to die. Maybe if Woody had received medical help right away, he would have lived. They're all responsible, everyone who participated in the plot."

"No one can say you are wrong, Señora. But accidents will happen. Who knows what God is thinking when he takes a life? The men, they were promised money. No one was to be hurt. Just hold them a few days, get money from the rich American, and let them go. They are very upset now. They have to take care of the tall one, and they have no money. They don't want to harm him. They only want what they were promised."

"Are you telling me that kidnapping wasn't their idea to begin with, that someone paid them to hijack Woody and Vaughan?"

"But that is just the problem, Señora. They have not been paid. These men, they are not the professional criminals like the ones in the big cities. They are simple people. They try to provide for their families. It is just the way things are. Sometimes temptation is too much to resist. It is sad, but it is true. It was not their idea to kidnap anyone. El Grande, he convinced them no one would be hurt and there would be money enough for everyone."

"And who is El Grande?"

"This they did not tell me."

"Did they tell you where they were holding Vaughan Buckley? Can you take me to him?"

"That is why I am here."

"When can we go?"

"It is too soon," he said. "We wait till the guards are gone, till our friend, he takes his turn at watch. He will pretend to sleep, and we can rescue your friend."

Maria Elena's worries came immediately to mind. "How do I know I can trust you?" I said. "How do I know you aren't using this as a ruse to kidnap me and hold me for ransom as well?"

"You are wise to be suspicious. And I can only assure you of my good intentions, and my hopes for your friend to be restored to the bosom of his loving family, just as you have preserved the family of the balloon seller."

I studied his face. There was kindness in the eyes and sadness, too, a resignation to the evils of mankind and an understanding of the forces that generated them. "Who are you?" I asked, although I suspected I knew.

"One who would help my people."

"And your people are all people."

He nodded.

"Thank you, Father," I said.

He smiled. "You are welcome, my child."

Chapter Twenty-two

An hour later, Father Alfredo and I quit the bar. I was grateful to escape the smoke, the jovial crowd, even the lively music, to step outside and breathe in the damp night air. On any other occasion, I would have enjoyed La Filomela. A melting pot of San Miguel where tourists and natives alike mingled, it presented an opportunity to meet friendly people and soak up the musical culture of the city in an informal, unceremonious atmosphere.

Tonight, however, I was anxious to leave. Even as patrons trooped in with bulky cases holding musical instruments and formed impromptu ensembles to perform together, even as they passed around their instruments to others eager to take a turn playing, and even after discovering that the priest himself played guitar and sang traditional songs in a hearty baritone, nothing could draw my mind from Vaughan, from the need to find him before his captors lost patience and took out their frustration on him. I wanted to free him, to bring him safely home to Olga's arms.

"I am glad you had the opportunity to see a little of our musical heritage," Father Alfredo said as he guided me past a group of men lingering outside the cantina. "Perhaps you can take home some nice memories of Mexico, not only the bad ones."

"Mexico is a beautiful country," I said, "and there's a lot to admire in this city and its people. But I'm afraid I really couldn't concentrate this evening on what it has to offer."

"I understand," he said. "However, we needed to wait. Much nicer to pass the time with music and friends than to cower in the dark till the change of watch takes place. You will grant me that, no?"

I smiled. "You'll get no argument from me."

We turned off the cantina's street and wandered down a cobblestone mews. In the narrow passage the buildings loomed over us, their roofs seeming to reach out for each other. Father Alfredo took my arm. "Watch your footing here," he said. "It is difficult to see."

There were no streetlights in this part of the city, but once my eyes became accustomed to the gloom, I could make out a few details. We were in an area of San Miguel where the buildings showed signs of age, with patches of stucco and paint having fallen away, and metal balconies rusted, in some cases barely attached to the wall. Large cracks in foundations became homes for straggly weeds. Overhead, laundry lines were strung from window to window, a few with forgotten items hanging stiffly. We skirted baby carriages, bicycles, and shopping carts left in the street, passed an old man sitting on a battered wooden chair smoking, and greeted a group of teenagers gathered on a corner, teasing each other. Sounds from open windows drifted over us, the peculiar warble of a television program, voices calling to each other, a couple arguing, a baby crying, a woman singing, laughter, music, and conversation. Life in this neighborhood was lived in full view, often on the street, not behind closed doors and in elegant courtyards as it was in the Buckleys' more affluent part of town.

We entered a broader avenue, which appeared to be an industrial area. The buildings were spaced farther apart, one story now instead of two, some with chain-link fences girding them. The ground beneath our feet was no longer paved, the hard-packed dirt easier to walk on. There were no sidewalks. An unseen drunk started singing loudly. A dog howled in reply. I looked over my shoulder to see the man lurch across the street toward an open doorway. Father Alfredo hummed softly to himself.

"Which building are we going to?" I asked.

He cocked his head and lowered his voice. "See the brick one over there, the one with the fence?"

"Have you been in this building before?"

He shook his head.

"Do you know its layout?"

Another shake.

"How will we get in?" I asked.

"I have the key for the gate," he said, reaching in the pocket of his black slacks.

"Do you need a flashlight?" I asked. "I have one in my purse."

"Hold on to it. You may need it yourself. I will go first. If I am seen, I will step forward to talk to them. You stay in the shadows. They must not see you. Once we are certain it is our friend who is on guard duty, we proceed. If not, we must abandon the scheme. It will be too dangerous otherwise."

This time it was my turn to shake my head. "I'm not leaving here without Vaughan," I said. "I'll sneak around the back and see if there's a way in from there. I'll signal to you if I find anything. If it's not our friend on duty and the guard is alert enough to catch you, engage him in a discussion, create a diversion while I look for Vaughan."

"It is not safe for you," he said.

"It's not safe for you, either," I replied. "We're partners in this project, are we not?"

He gave me a rueful smile. "Are all American women so difficult?" he said.

"I can't speak for all American women," I said. "I'm not difficult, just determined."

We had walked beyond the structure to get a wide-angle view of the property. In addition to the main building, there was a large wooden shed with barn doors. A patch of weeds ran along one side. We turned back to approach the building from the other direction. It was completely dark. Not even a slit of light showed near the metal door, and the windows were black, the glass panes painted to prevent anyone from peering in.

Father Alfredo inserted his key into the padlock on the gate. To our sensitive ears, the sharp click as the lock released sounded like a gunshot in the quiet night. We froze in place, hardly daring to breathe, fearing the noise would alert the watchman and set the dog to howling again. But no one responded, including the dog.

We allowed ourselves to breathe again. Father Alfredo opened the gate little by little, testing for squeaks and leaving barely enough room for us to slip inside the property. He slid his body through and motioned for me to follow. I put my foot inside the gap, holding the gate with both hands to make sure it didn't move and sound a warning. Once through, I let go of the gate, but my jacket pocket caught on the hasp, jerking me back roughly. A gasp escaped my lips. Father Alfredo turned, a finger to his lips. Seeing my predicament, he gently extricated the fabric from the metal strap.

Once through the gate, we crept into the shadows of the shed. Father Alfredo tried again to convince me to hide, pointing to the front door and then to himself, and indicating the far side of the shed where he wanted me to go. We argued silently, me shaking my head and making a circle with my finger to show him I would go around to the back. Eventually he gave up. Cautioning me to be on alert, he moved slowly toward the door, gingerly planting one foot after the other in the gravel and dirt to muffle the sound of his footfalls.

I made my move, too, using the swath of weeds alongside the shed to steal quietly to the rear of the building. My eyes, now more accustomed to the dark, surveyed the terrain. The building had a concrete loading dock with several doors to the interior. I climbed up onto the platform. Other than a pile of scrap lumber and a stack of two-by-fours, the dock was bare. I pressed my ear to the first door and tried to discern any sounds inside. I heard nothing. Holding my breath, I slowly tried the doorknob, hoping someone had been lax enough to leave the door unlocked. No luck. I checked each door in succession, listening first, then trying the knob. At the last door, I detected a shuffling noise inside. It seemed to be coming closer. I grabbed a four-foot length of board and hurried back, positioning myself to the side of the door away from where it would open, my back pressed against the wall. Had they discovered Father Alfredo? Were they questioning him, pressuring him? Did they suspect he came with an accomplice and intend to look for me?

The sounds from inside grew louder. Something heavy was being shoved along the floor. I could hear the scrape of its movement. There was a crash, and a muffled growl. Whoever it was fell against the door and rattled the doorknob. Then I heard the snick of the lock. I raised the board over my head as the door slowly opened.

"Señora, are you there?" a voice called. It was Father Alfredo.

I dropped my arms and heaved a sigh of relief. "You were almost a victim yourself, Father," I said, cocking my head toward my would-be weapon.

"I'm glad you thought to wait before swinging," he said. "Come inside. There's no one here."

"No one? No guard? No Vaughan?"

"Not that I could find. The place is deserted. But watch out—there are boxes everywhere."

I followed him through the door, reached in my bag for my flashlight, and shined the beam around the space. Wooden crates and stacks of cardboard boxes were scattered across the floor. I pulled aside the straw in an open crate to see a colorful hand-painted ceramic sink. A brief search revealed boxes of handmade crafts—plates and pitchers, clay bird rattles, marionettes dressed like Mexican peasants, pierced metal frames, papier-mâché masks, wooden maracas, tissue-paper piñatas—waiting to be crated for shipment.

"Are you sure no one is here?" I asked.

"They are not here now. Whether they will be back at any moment, I cannot tell."

"And no sign of Vaughan?"

He shook his head sadly. "I am sorry, Señora."

I wandered the room. One side was clearly a packing area. Hammers, crowbars, and other tools dangled from nails tapped into the wall. Crates sat empty next to bales of straw. New and half-used rolls of packing tape were threaded on a dowel. Near the front door, I found a light switch. I flipped it up and three widely spaced fixtures— really just bare bulbs—came to life, spilling dim pools of light on the warehouse floor. To my right, two chairs and a table sat next to a large garbage can, the top of which had been left off. A half-empty liquor bottle sat on the floor.

"Are you sure we should turn on the light? Maybe they were never here. Maybe this is the wrong building," Father Alfredo said, looking around uncertainly. "We are not here legally, and we don't want to be noticed."

"The key opened the gate," I said. "How did you get in the building?"

"The door was unlocked."

"Then we must be in the right place," I said. "And if I'm not mistaken, someone was here recently." I leaned over the garbage can and aimed the flashlight to examine its contents.

"What have you found?"

"Leftover food. It hasn't been here very long."

"How can you tell?"

"It doesn't smell bad yet, but I'm afraid if you leave the top off overnight, you'll notice quite a difference in the morning."

Father Alfredo clicked his tongue. "They're going to draw rats with this garbage."

"They may have already," I said, angling my head to catch a soft scratching sound. I swung the beam of my flashlight around the perimeter of the room, looking for an indication of rodents.

Father Alfredo shuddered. "I am very brave with people," he said, "but I do not like rats. I think we should go."

"I realize you're concerned about our being discovered

here," I said. "You can wait outside if it will make you feel better. I just need a little more time."

"No. No, I would never think to leave you alone."

"That's very kind of you," I said, smiling at him. I put my shoulder bag and flashlight on the table and examined each of the chairs, running my fingers over the rough wooden rails on the top and sides. "I'll only be a minute more."

"What are you looking for?"

"Fibers. Hairs. Any evidence that indicates Vaughan was here—and I think I may have found it."

Father Alfredo drew closer and squinted at the chair. "I don't see anything."

"There's something sticky on this chair."

"Why is that important? Someone with dirty hands, maybe from the food?"

I sniffed at the chair. "It's not food," I said. "And it's on both sides. It could be adhesive from packing tape."

"To repair the chair?"

"It doesn't look as if it's been repaired," I said, "but they might have used the tape to keep someone in the seat."

I retrieved my flashlight and swung it from side to side, box to box. The floor was littered with fragments of straw. I spotted several bales stacked on a pallet, ready to be packed around goods.

"I think I hear the rats," he said. "Do you see them?"

"The packing area is over here," I said, pointing the beam at the bales. "Why is there a pile of straw down there?" The straw lay beside several wooden crates that looked as if they had been hammered shut, ready for shipping.

"Maybe someone has been stealing some of the goods," he said. "Or maybe that's where the rats—they are making a nest. We must go. I have a bad feeling here."

"I wonder," I said, walking away from him to examine the pattern of straw on the floor. "Look," I said. "The fragments of straw are pretty evenly distributed, but here something was dragged through it. See these lines that lead from the table?"

"The boxes, they are heavy. Maybe the men pushed one out of the way. I had to do that to get to the back door."

"Show me where you moved the box," I said.

"Certainly." He walked toward the door we'd used to enter the warehouse and gazed around to get his bearings. "This is the one," he said, patting the top of a wooden case. "I'm sure of it. I stubbed my foot on this corner."

The light was too diffuse to see clearly. I knelt down, training my flashlight on the floor and the edge of the crate. "The pattern here is different," I said. "Over there are two parallel lines. Here's a clear patch where the bottom of the crate pushed the straw away." I walked back to the lines in the straw at the other end of the room.

"You are a very observant woman. This is good," Father Alfredo said. "It is time to go now. Yes?"

I took a rough measurement of the space between the lines and went back to the chairs. The distance between the lines matched the space between the two back legs of the chair.

"They dragged the chair over there," I said softly to myself. "It must be because it was too heavy to lift." I followed the lines. "A box would make a much broader mark in the straw," I mused. "These lines go to the crates in the corner."

"Señora?"

I put one finger up to ask him to wait, as my eyes went to where the chair had been dragged. "There's only one set of marks. I suppose the chair must have been carried back to the table. It would have been lighter then."

"Señora, it is getting late."

"I'll be right with you," I said, "but let me take a look at those crates first."

"All right, but please hurry."

I grabbed a crowbar that had been left in the packing area.

"We don't need to open them, do we?" he said, following me.

"That noise we heard earlier was coming from somewhere around here," I said, tapping on a crate.

"Why do you want to disturb the rats? I think we should leave them alone."

I peered at the tops of the crates. "There," I said, pointing to a crate hemmed in by three others. "On the front ones, there's only one set of nails, but on that one, you can see the nails and holes where they were removed once."

"Why can't we just open this one? It's closer."

Using all my strength, I attempted to shove one of the crates out of the way, unmindful of the racket it made as the wood scraped against the stone floor. It barely budged.

"Careful now. You will hurt your back. That's too heavy for you," he said. "I'll help you." We pressed our weight against the rough wooden slats until, one by one, we were able to wrestle the crates aside and gain access to the one I wanted.

I took the crowbar and wedged it under the corner of the top where it had been hammered shut. "Let's get this open," I said.

"Let me," Father Alfredo said, taking over and levering the bar enough to release the nails with a loud squeal.

"Now this side," I said. I could no longer hear the scratching, but I was certain this was the right crate.

Father Alfredo jammed the crowbar under the opposite corner. "I think I have it now."

We managed to lift the top a few inches, but it was too dark to see inside the crate.

"It needs to come off," I said.

"I hope you know what you're doing." Father Alfredo maneuvered to the other side of the crate and repeated the work with the crowbar. When the last nail gave up its hold with a sigh, the top was freed. He pulled it off and flung it aside; it landed with a noisy clatter on the floor.

I leaned over the side of the crate and directed my flashlight inside. A heavy blanket concealed the contents. I reached in and pulled up a corner of it.

"*Madre de Dios,*" Father Alfredo said, crossing himself.

He was curled in the bottom of the crate, his eyes shut, his clothes filthy, flecked with straw and I didn't want to think what else, hands and feet bound with tape. His hair, usually so neatly groomed, was dusty and stood away from his scalp in spikes. His mouth was sealed with more tape, the plastic close in hue to the deathly pallor of his mottled skin and the stubble of whiskers that shadowed his gaunt cheeks.

"Is he alive?" Father Alfredo whispered.

"Vaughan?" I said softly.

He opened his eyes.

Chapter Twenty-three

It took all our strength to lift Vaughan out of the crate. I carried over a chair from the table, the same one in which he'd been bound, then dragged to his wooden prison. He slumped in the seat, his eyes closed, while we worked to release his bindings and delicately tear away the tape covering his mouth. Father Alfredo's face was a mask of grief as he silently ministered to Vaughan, patiently cutting away the hair where the adhesive pulled at his skin to spare him the pain of ripping the tape off, rubbing his ankles and calves, then his shoulders, arms, and wrists to revive the circulation as each limb was released.

Vaughn took in a deep breath through his mouth when the last bit of tape was removed. Father Alfredo retrieved the liquor bottle we'd found next to the garbage can. "We have no medicine," he said, "but this may prevent infection." He dabbed alcohol on Vaughan's wrists where the tape had abraded his skin.

"Ouch, that stings," Vaughan croaked. "I think I'd be better off drinking it."

Father Alfredo offered him the bottle. Vaughan shook his head and gave a slight snort. "Not unless you have a straw." He gestured to his lips, which were cracked and bleeding. "But I thank you, sir."

I watched the exchange, silently assessing Vaughan's condition. Dark circles ringed his eyes, and I was sure every muscle in his body was sore. He was exhausted from lack of sleep, but his sense of humor was undamaged. He turned to me. "Ah, Jessica," he said. "I had faith you would find me. But the heroines in your books work a lot faster. What took you so long?"

"It is God who has led her to you," Father Alfredo said.

"No doubt," Vaughan said, taking note of the priest. "I don't believe we've met."

I introduced them. "Father Alfredo helped me find you, Vaughan, but we need to get you out of here before the kidnappers come back," I said. "Do you think you can stand?"

"Not yet," Vaughan said, rubbing an aching shoulder. "But I doubt they'll be back. My Spanish isn't great, but I pieced together what they said. They were locking me up to give themselves time to get away. They were afraid the police were right behind them."

"I hope this is true, that the authorities find them," Father Alfredo said. "I am very angry. I was deceived. This was not what I expected to find. The men, they say they are not criminals. But this"—he pointed to Vaughan—"this is inexcusable. To be poor is not a crime, to struggle and take desperate measures to feed your family, this is regrettable but understandable. But to treat the life of another as if it has no value, to tie him up and leave him like an animal going to slaughter, that is criminal. I am ashamed of myself for believing they were doing no great harm."

"Not your fault, Father," Vaughan said. "I was just in the wrong place at the wrong time." He looked at me, his eyes questioning. "Did Woody make it?" he asked.

I shook my head.

His chin dropped to his chest. "I was afraid of that. The damned fool, waving that gun around."

"What happened there? Do you remember?"

"We were delayed getting back. We were supposed to get an early start and be home before dark, but Woody got into a hassle over the hotel bill with some guy who spoke no English. I told him we should just pay it and get on the road, but he insisted we were getting cheated. We had to wait around for the manager to arrive before it could be resolved. And, of course, the charge was legitimate. The manager was very accommodating—he even paid for our breakfast—but he was correct. We owed the money. Woody kept arguing until I pulled him away. By that time it was almost noon." He sighed and rubbed his eyes. "I think I'd like to try to get up now."

Father Alfredo and I each took an arm and assisted Vaughan to his feet. He swayed momentarily, then gained his balance and straightened up. "That feels good," he said, taking a deep breath.

We supported him, walking in a small circle around the

chair and holding his arms, till he shook us off. He took a few steps by himself before his legs gave out. Father Alfredo and I jumped forward, catching him before he fell and putting him back in the seat.

"Darn legs fell asleep, cramped in that box. They're still tingling."

"Give yourself a little more time," I said.

"I'll be fine once the blood in my legs starts pumping again." He rubbed his thighs with his palms.

Father Alfredo drew me aside. "I'm going to check outside to make sure we are still alone," he said.

"Be careful," I said. "I'm not entirely convinced they won't return."

"I am of the same mind. If they do, I will signal to you to give you time to take your friend out the rear door." He went to Vaughan and patted his shoulder. "You rest," he said. "We will try to get you moving again soon."

"Thank you, Father," Vaughan said.

The priest slipped out the front door and closed it silently behind him. I turned to Vaughan. He was fading, the excitement of being rescued giving way to the exhaustion of having reached the end of his ordeal. He drowsed in the chair, but I couldn't let him fall asleep. Staying in the warehouse was not an option. We needed to get him home.

I shook Vaughan's shoulder.

"I'm awake," he said. "I'm just thinking about Woody."

"Let's try walking again," I said. "You can tell me more of what happened."

He leaned on my arm and stood, taking small shuffling steps until he felt more secure on his legs.

"Tell me something," I said. "Olga thought you would call if you were going to be late. If you had, I'm sure she would have insisted you stay away another day rather than risk the road after sunset."

"Oh, my sweet Olga," he said, smiling for the first time. "She warned me not to go. I meant to call home, wanted to, but Woody refused to stop. He kept insisting he could make up the time. And the cell phones were useless in the mountains." He leaned heavily against me and closed his eyes. I thought he might fall asleep standing up.

"Talk to me, Vaughan," I prompted him. "Tell me about the kidnapping. How did that happen?"

He opened his eyes. "I'm not sure." He took a few tentative steps and stopped again. "We came upon an accident, at least that's what we thought it was. Somebody lying in the middle of the road. Woody pulled over to help, and they jumped us."

"How many were there?"

"Four men. They seemed to be arguing about what they were doing. I thought they were going to let us go. Then Woody got into a scuffle with one of them. He drew his gun and this guy jumped on him, trying to wrestle it away. I heard a shot and Woody fell down."

"So it was Woody's own gun that killed him?"

"Yes. I don't even know if the men were armed."

"What happened then?"

"It's a little hazy now. I think I screamed at the men to

get help. I tried to stem the bleeding, but all I had was Olga's handkerchief." He looked down at his hands as if still seeing the blood. "I threw it under the car. One of them must have knocked me unconscious. That's all I can remember till I woke up in here with a blindfold over my eyes and a lump the size of Central Park." He probed the back of his head with his fingers. "It still feels pretty swollen."

"How long were you in the crate?" I asked, urging him to walk again. "Did they keep you there the whole time they had you?"

"No. Most of the time I was tied to a chair, listening to them arguing about what to do with me."

"Did they feed you?"

"Sometimes. I wasn't very hungry. I kept thinking about Woody, hoping he got help, and worrying about Olga, sure she was worrying about me." His steps were getting stronger as we circled the warehouse.

"Did you know Woody was carrying a gun?"

"I had no idea. I like to think I wouldn't have gone with him had I known that—we've always been very much against guns, Olga and I—but I can't honestly say that's true. I wanted to go. He made the trip sound like something only brave young men undertake, a great adventure."

"And was it?"

"Not really. He handed me a bill of goods. I think he just wanted company. It's a long, mostly boring drive. Of course, it ended up being more of an adventure than either of us bargained for." Vaughan shook his head. "He acted like a cowboy, waving that gun around. I told him to calm down and do whatever they asked. But he wouldn't listen. I can't figure out why. He liked to fancy himself a macho man. Maybe it was the influence of the Mexican culture. Maybe he just missed the excitement of his military career or wanted to relive his youth. I remember thinking at the time that he knew what he was doing. I was admiring him. Until, of course, he got shot."

"Did he say anything to you after he was hit?"

"No. I kept talking to him, but he didn't respond. He was unconscious. Maybe he was already dead. I don't know. I just remember yelling. Yelling at the men. Yelling at Woody. And then everything went black."

Father Alfredo had returned while we'd been making the rounds of the room. He stood near the door, quietly listening to Vaughan's story. We stopped in front of him. He took Vaughan's hand and patted it. "God has spared you," he said. "I will pray for you tonight, and for the souls of the men who mistreated you."

"Thank you, Father."

"Did you see anything outside?" I asked.

"It was quiet. I think we should try to leave," he said.

"Yes," I said, turning to Vaughan. "I'll feel a lot better once we have you home and we can report back to the police. Do you think you can walk a short distance?"

"I'll try."

I pulled the strap of my bag over my shoulder, turned off the lights in the warehouse, and opened the door. We stepped outside into the cool night, pulling the door shut behind us. Something was not right. There was a hum in the air that hadn't been there earlier. I strained to see into the dark. My eyes had adjusted to the lights inside the building, and I couldn't see ahead of me.

"What is it, Jessica?" Vaughan whispered.

"I'm not sure," I whispered back.

We heard a click and a blinding searchlight poured over us, fixing us where we stood, as unable to move as butter-flies pinned to a board. I squinted against the glare, shield-ing my eyes with my arm, trying urgently to see beyond the perimeter of the brilliant whiteness. The light was followed by the sound of a dozen rifles being cocked. Vaughan and I huddled together. Father Alfredo began to pray behind us.

"Put your hands up." The voice coming through the bullhorn was speaking English. "And keep them up."

As we raised our hands, a uniformed man stepped out of the darkness into the pool of light. It was Captain Gutierrez.

"Oh, thank goodness, it's you," I said.

Gutierrez touched a finger to his cap. "Señora Fletcher. I did not think to find you here." He gestured for us to put our hands down. "Padre." He nodded to Father Alfredo. "I see we are too late to rescue Señor Buckley."

"On the contrary," I said. "You're just in time. We want to get him home. His wife will be waiting, I'm sure."

Ignoring me, Gutierrez addressed Vaughan. "My apolo-gies for your suffering, Señor," he said. "I am Captain Gutierrez."

"Captain," Vaughan said, "I am very pleased to see you."

"May I escort you to the car?"

"Thank you," Vaughan said. "I would appreciate that."

Gutierrez assisted Vaughan to the patrol car, glancing back to give me a puzzled look. He helped him into the front passenger seat, then held the rear door open for Father Alfredo and me. The driver was one of the men we'd seen outside the cantina.

The captain closed the door and bent down to talk through the open window. "My officer will drive you home. Tomorrow, when you are refreshed, we will come to your home to ask you some questions."

"I appreciate your consideration," Vaughan said. "I'll be happy to talk to you then."

"I can assure you, Señor, we will find out who is responsible for this."

I leaned forward. "Captain?"

"Sí, Señora?"

"I think I can help you there."

Chapter Twenty-four

Word travels quickly in San Miguel de Allende. The following day the house began to fill up as friends and acquaintances crowded in to welcome Vaughan back. Bearing all manner of Mexican dishes that I recognized—tostadas, tamales, enchiladas, fajitas, sweet empanadas, wedding cookies, and flan—and even more that I didn't but that looked delicious, they filed into the house, depositing their gifts in the kitchen with Maria Elena. In short order the dining room table was laden with dishes and platters and trays of food, and as many as possible of the bouquets of flowers that had been arriving every hour, it seemed.

Olga had greeted Vaughan's return the night before with ecstatic exclamations, embraces, tears of joy, and palpable anxiety about his condition. He had refused her appeals that they call a doctor, saying all he wanted was a hot bath and a good meal. After effusively thanking everyone—the police, Father Alfredo, Maria Elena, and me—and urg-

ing us to help ourselves to food and drink, Olga had ushered Vaughan upstairs to their suite, where she'd run a
steamy bath for him, and as he'd soaked, plied him with
more food than the poor man could possibly consume,
along with pots of tea that she'd spiked heavily with brandy.
She'd thrown out his soiled clothing, made a fire in the bedroom fireplace, and used an old-fashioned iron warmer to
heat the sheets so that the bed would be cozy and comforting when he climbed beneath the covers. Her ministrations
and a good night's sleep had done wonders for her husband, who, looking refreshed, came downstairs in the
morning to an enormous breakfast and a continuous welcoming reception from San Miguel.

The church bells had sounded longer than usual, a
mark that the celebrant at La Parroquia had learned the
news. The mayor came to the house in person this time, together with a photographer, to pump Vaughan's hand, con-
gratulate him on his courage, and present him with the key
to the city. The editor of *Noticias* showed up with his own
camera to take a few pictures, jot down a few quotes, and
obtain the promise of a longer interview once Vaughan felt
up to it. He accepted an invitation to stay and share in the
festivities. A television station in Mexico City sent a camera
crew who wanted to film Vaughan back at the warehouse,
but Olga put her foot down. The TV reporter had to content himself with filing his story standing in the courtyard
in front of the house.

Arm slung around Olga's shoulder, Vaughan spent
most of the morning on the telephone with the press, and

also with well-wishers and friends from New York and elsewhere in the States, all giddy with delight at his rescue.

"No, no, I'm fine," I heard him say. "Jessica found me. I don't know. I haven't even had a chance to ask her. Yes, she's a good friend as well as a bestselling writer." He waved at me. "Not at all. We have no plans to sell our house in San Miguel. We love it here." He winked at Olga. "Well, the first order of business is to improve my Spanish. Yes, it would have been helpful to speak with my captors, or at least to be able to understand more of what they were saying. . . . No, I don't think they spoke any English. . . . Well, I listened, and I was able to make out some of the discussion, but I didn't try out my rudimentary Spanish. For one thing, I didn't want to discourage them from talking in front of me."

It was wonderful to see him happy. He was thinner and there were still traces of the pallor that had suffused his face when we'd found him, but he was visibly relaxed, relieved to be in familiar surroundings, even jovial in recounting his misadventures. In fact, I thought I detected a hint of him basking in all the hoopla and attention that attended his homecoming.

"I hadn't thought about writing a book, but maybe that's not such a bad idea," he told a publishing colleague. "Olga, sweetheart, please make a note about that. I'll have to get back to you on that, Dan. But if Signet thinks it's a good idea, Buckley House may entertain the notion."

They had rarely left each other's side. Olga had parked Vaughan on the sofa in the living room, sitting beside him and forming a human barrier to keep everyone at a safe distance. "Don't you dare get up when people come in," she said, frowning at him. "All that up and down will tire you out. No one will think you're being discourteous."

"I'm not an invalid, Olga. I'm feeling better by the minute."

"Humor me."

"I guess I'll have to," he said, taking her hand and kissing it. "I'm afraid you'll get violent if I disobey."

"It's a definite possibility," she replied with a smile. "Don't tempt me."

Dina pulled at my sleeve. "Isn't it exciting, Jessica? And so romantic. Roberto and I are thrilled he's safe."

Roberto's expression didn't match his wife's words. "I don't suppose you'll have time now to work with me on our book," he said.

"I'm afraid not," I said.

"It could have been a big bestseller, you know."

"Well, in that case," I said, "you should continue working on it. I'll be happy to read it when you're finished and, if you like, make some suggestions."

"I'd rather you gave it to your editor."

"Why don't you get it written first," I said.

"Roberto, did you see the buffet?" Dina asked, tugging her husband toward the dining room. "Excuse us, Jessica."

"You look pretty good, considering," Guy Kovach said to Vaughan. "Doesn't he?" he asked his wife, Nancy, as well as Cathie Harrison and Eric Gewirtz, who sat on the sofa across from the Buckleys.

"That's because you can't see the scars inside," Vaughan said.

"You're kidding, right?" Nancy said. "They didn't beat you or anything?"

"No. They decided tying me to a chair all day long and dumping me in a crate at night was sufficient torture."

"He's a lucky man," said Roberto, who rejoined us, balancing two plates of food. Dina put down her margarita to turn a desk chair around for her husband to sit. "You know the odds were against you," he said to Vaughan.

"They weren't going to hurt him till they got the money," Guy said. "You saved a bundle by getting rescued."

"He's worth more than all the money in the world to me," Olga said.

"I never thought of San Miguel as being dangerous," Cathie said, "or I wouldn't have brought my children here."

"There's no place without crime," Eric countered. "We've taught them to be cautious and not to trust strangers. And there's no chance they'll be driving after dark on these roads. You do what you can, and then you have to trust their judgment."

"This isn't Mexico City," Roberto said. "We have a pretty low crime rate, all in all."

"Except for theft," Dina put in.

"I've never had anything stolen," Nancy said.

Sarah entered the room, her expression serious. "Thank God," she said when she saw Vaughan. "I can't tell you how relieved I am to see you." There was none of the flirtatiousness that had marked her previous exchanges with him. "I prayed every day that the police would find you, and my prayers were answered."

"Actually, it was Jessica and Father Alfredo who found me," Vaughan said. "But thanks for your prayers. I'm grateful for all the concern about me and especially for all the support everyone gave Olga. I was more worried about her—and Woody—than about myself."

"Woody's funeral is tomorrow," Sarah said. "I hope you'll be able to make it."

"Without question, I'll be there. How is Philip?"

"He's doing okay. He's here somewhere."

"He is?"

"I brought him with me. He was glad to hear you were rescued."

Vaughan ignored Olga's instructions and struggled to his feet, his muscles still sore from his ordeal. "I'd like to talk with Philip," he told her.

"Of course," she said, taking his arm. "Let's go find him."

Sarah took Olga's place on the sofa. "You're quite the sleuth, I hear," she said to me.

"I've been lucky at times," I said.

"With the kind of luck you have," Guy said, "I'd like to take you to Las Vegas with me."

"Guy!" his wife said, but she flashed a smile at me.

"You can come too, Nancy. I wouldn't leave you home."

"Well, that's a relief."

Guy slapped his thighs. "That's a great-looking plate of food our friend Roberto has over there," he said. "I'm going to get something to eat. C'mon, Nancy."

The Kovachs went off to the dining room, and Cathie and Eric followed them.

Roberto waited till they were out of hearing range before commenting, "See? What did I tell you? He's always looking for the easy buck."

"Not now," his wife said, frowning into her empty glass.

Maria Elena came to me and whispered that Chief Rivera and Captain Gutierrez were in the courtyard.

I went to find them. "Chief Rivera, I hadn't realized you'd returned," I said, shaking his hand. "I'm happy to see you again."

"And I, Señora Fletcher, was very pleased to learn that your good friend has been found."

"He has, and thanks to Captain Gutierrez, he's safely at home."

"I understand from my captain that you have been very busy in my absence."

"Captain Gutierrez has been most helpful," I said, eyeing Gutierrez and daring him to contradict me.

"Is that so?"

"We were in a precarious position last night, in a deserted part of town, afraid the kidnappers might come back, and with no one to help us. If the captain hadn't turned up when he did, I don't know what would have happened." I smiled at Gutierrez.

"Señora," the captain said, nodding at me. His face was set in a scowl. I had thought we might have come to some kind of acceptance after the previous night, but it was not to be. Captain Gutierrez wasn't about to drop his macho façade, no matter what.

Rivera smiled. "I didn't hear the story quite the same way."

"Come in and join the welcome home party," I said. "Everyone is so grateful for Vaughan's safe recovery."

They followed me inside.

"You know we finally traced the murder weapon," Rivera said. "The gun belonged—"

"To Woody," I said, finishing his sentence. "Yes, I know."

Rivera's eyebrows shot up.

"You see?" Gutierrez said.

Vaughan was back on the couch. The day's social activities had taken an obvious toll. He was drawn, and the dark crescents under his eyes that a good night's sleep had softened were starting to reappear. He perked up at the sight of the policemen, however, and stood to greet them.

"Señor Buckley, it's a pleasure to meet you," Chief Rivera said after I'd introduced them.

"The pleasure is mine," Vaughan replied. He shook hands with Gutierrez. "Good of you to come."

"Actually," Rivera said, "we're here on official business."

"I thought you might be," Vaughan said. "Would you like to go upstairs to my study where it's quiet?"

"I don't think so." Rivera raised his eyebrows at me. "Señora Fletcher, my colleague informs me that you might have some knowledge to contribute about the crime. If that's the case, I would like to hear it."

"I do have a theory," I said. "After talking with Father

Alfredo last night, I'm convinced the men responsible for the kidnapping were simply hired thugs, working for someone else."

"Who would that person be?" Rivera asked.

"It had to be someone who not only knew that the mail run was going to take place but also knew the precise timetable."

"That could be anyone in this room," Guy said.

"Yes, it could."

"You're not accusing one of us, Jessica, are you?" Sarah asked.

I didn't answer, letting the silence speak, and looking at each person in turn. My eyes rested on Roberto.

He was visibly nervous. "Buckley and I haven't always gotten along," he said, "but that doesn't mean I had anything to do with this."

"They're not accusing you," Dina said. "Roberto would never hurt anyone, would you, Bob?"

"Shut up, Dina."

She closed her eyes momentarily, then got up and walked away.

Philip had come into the room after the police had arrived, followed by the editor of *Noticias,* but they kept their distance from the others, Philip obviously uncomfortable among his father's friends and Guillermo Sylva reluctant to draw attention to himself and possibly be asked to leave. Maria Elena and Hector stood in the doorway.

Philip spoke up. "You don't think those men were just bandits waiting for whoever showed up?"

"No, I don't," I said. "They were waiting for Woody and Vaughan. They knew they would be returning, and they had a good idea what time it would be."

"That should cut down the number of people with inside knowledge, Jessica," Vaughan said. "I called Olga, so I presume you and Maria Elena knew we were on our way home. Woody must have called Philip. Am I right, Philip?"

"Yes."

"Did you tell anyone?" Vaughan asked.

"That my father was on his way back? I—I don't know. I might have mentioned it to a few friends. That doesn't mean they were involved. I told you, too, Sarah, didn't I? Did you tell anyone?"

"No. I don't believe I spoke with anyone about it. No offense, but it wasn't something of great interest. Woody went on mail runs all the time."

"How do you know," Captain Gutierrez asked me, "that these criminals were waiting to ambush Señor Manheim and Señor Buckley?"

"Father Alfredo told me that they had been recruited by a man they called El Grande."

"El Grande? That's funny," Nancy said. "That means 'the big one.' That's what they call Guy at the local market. Got to watch that tummy, hon."

Her husband glared at her. She gasped and clapped her hand over her mouth. "No, no, it couldn't have been Guy," she said. "We had no idea when Vaughan and Woody would be back."

"No, we didn't," Guy confirmed, his face grim.

"The padre, he knows who these men are?" Gutierrez asked.

"If he does, he'll never tell you," Vaughan said.

"Why not?" Nancy asked.

"He would likely claim the sanctity of the confessional," I said. "Whatever he learns when someone goes to confession must be kept strictly confidential. That's a rule of the Church. If he breaks that rule, he could face excommunication."

"But what if what he found out about them wasn't from confession?" Philip asked.

"I don't know if he knows who they are," I said, "or has only heard about them secondhand. Another man was supposed to participate in the kidnapping, but he backed out at the last minute."

"At least there was one smart one," Roberto said.

"It was this man's replacement who shot Woody, according to Father Alfredo. He said he was told it wasn't supposed to happen that way. It was supposed to be a kidnapping for money, with no one hurt."

"So, who hired the men?" Sarah asked.

I met her eyes and waited to see if she would look away. "Don't you know?" I asked.

"Me?" Her voice was shrill. "Why would I know?"

"Because you wrote the note that was delivered to the newspaper the night of the kidnapping. And you sent an instant message to Olga demanding the ransom, knowing it would be me or Maria Elena reading it, since you were at the house when Olga left for the airport."

Sarah laughed. "You have a fanciful imagination, Jessica. You've been writing too many novels. Woody and I were friends. Why would I kill him?"

"I didn't say you killed him. I said you wrote the message that was published in *Noticias*, the one that resulted in banner headlines about the kidnapping. You jumped the gun by sending the message in early. I guess you didn't want to be late for your gallery opening. As a result, the editor knew about the kidnapping before Olga or the police did."

"That's ridiculous," Sarah said. "You're making it up. I'd like to see you prove such allegations."

"So would I," Rivera muttered.

"It shouldn't be too hard," I said, turning to the editor. "The letter you received, Señor Sylva. What distinguishing characteristic did it have?"

"You mean the ink smudge on the corner?"

"Yes. And what color was it?" I asked.

"Blue. It was blue ink."

I turned back to Sarah. "The day I met you, your fingers were stained with blue ink. Yesterday, when I visited your studio, you warned me about the ink being permanent. You showed me the blue stains on your smock."

Sarah smiled, but her eyes were hard. "So what?" she said defiantly. "Lots of artists use ink in their work. I've been experimenting with a new medium. That doesn't make me a criminal."

"I imagine if the police want to compare the fingerprints they found on the letter with yours, they would find a match. Here is your rebel leader, Chief Rivera. No wonder the soldiers have had a hard time finding the revolutionaries. They never thought to look under their noses at an artist who puts her political beliefs in her paintings."

Captain Gutierrez grabbed Sarah's wrist. "I think you had better come with me, Señorita. We have some questions."

Sarah pulled her hand away. "My father's a lawyer. You'll never get away with this."

"Hold up a minute," Chief Rivera said. "Don't tell me this is El Grande. Are you saying she hired those men to kill Señor Manheim?"

"No," I replied. "She didn't. Woody's death was an accident. He was showing off for Vaughan, challenging the men. He didn't realize that one of them was not in on the playacting. The gun that killed him was his own."

"Then who is El Grande?"

I gazed around the room, taking in the taut faces of those in attendance—Vaughan and Olga, Chief Rivera, Captain Gutierrez, Roberto and Dina Fisher, Guillermo Sylva, Guy and Nancy Kovach, Cathie, Eric, Maria Elena and her brother Hector, Sarah. My eyes came to rest on Philip. "I'm sorry, Philip," I said. "El Grande was your father."

There was a shocked pause and then everyone started to talk at once. Only Sarah remained silent, her eyes distraught, watching the tears roll down Philip's cheeks.

"I knew it. I just knew it," Philip sobbed.

Chapter Twenty-five

"The poor fool," Vaughan said, leaning back in his lounge chair under the colonnade. "I can't believe he ended up, in effect, arranging for his own death."

It was another beautiful day in San Miguel de Allende, the sun shining, the church bells ringing, the birds singing in the acacia tree in the courtyard. Vaughan, Olga, and I had been sipping our morning coffee, reading the special edition of *Noticias*, reviewing the events of the previous day, and making plans for the future.

"It looks like he intended to share part of the money with the kidnappers," I said, "give Sarah what she needed to keep the Revolutionary Guanajuato Brigade well funded, and have enough left over to send Philip back to college."

"I guess a military pension doesn't afford much more than a modest lifestyle, even here in Mexico," Olga said. "He seemed like such a nice man . . ."

Vaughan raised one eyebrow and peered at his wife.

"Even if I couldn't bear to be around him," she finished.

"He had been leading a double life for a long time," I said.

"What tipped you off?" Vaughan asked.

"Roberto talked about people living in San Miguel and never learning Spanish. I thought it strange that a man who had been in military intelligence, like Woody, would settle in a country and not speak the language. And Olga, you confirmed that for me."

"I did."

"Yes. The man you met with in New York, the one from the State Department, knew Woody from an assignment in Mexico."

"That's right, Jessica. I remember thinking it was typical military *un*intelligence, sending an operative who didn't speak Spanish to Mexico."

"Exactly. And while our government makes a lot of mistakes, that wouldn't have been one of them," I said. "When I was at Woody's apartment, I looked at his e-mail. Half the messages were in Spanish, as were his replies. And a local bookstore sent him a postcard saying the book he ordered was available. It was a book on military operations—and the title was in Spanish."

"So the sign on his car saying he didn't speak Spanish was all part of this elaborate ruse to keep people from knowing he did," Vaughan said. "Why would he bother?"

"People in intelligence often get so involved in living undercover, they find it difficult to break away, even after the operation is over."

"I wonder what he did for American intelligence here?" Olga mused.

"He infiltrated revolutionary cells," said a deep voice.

We all looked up to see Chief Rivera walking toward us across the courtyard.

"Maria Elena let me in on her way out. I hope you don't mind if I join you this morning," he said. "I have some lingering questions of my own."

"Not at all, Chief," Vaughan said, rising. "Can we get you some coffee?"

"I wouldn't say no," Rivera said, taking a chair.

Vaughan went into the kitchen and returned with a steaming mug.

"I tried to talk Maria Elena into staying and having coffee with us," Olga said, "but she said she was going to La Parroquia to give thanks for Vaughan's return and, not incidentally, to thank Father Alfredo for his part in the rescue. I asked her to invite him to dinner. You're welcome to come, too."

"*Gracias,*" Rivera said. "Please ask me another time. My son has a baseball game this afternoon, and we're all going out to dinner to celebrate his team's victory, whether they win or not. By the way, I thought you'd want to know Gutierrez picked up some men in the warehouse district, who we believe might be our kidnappers. He's questioning them now."

Vaughan blew out a long breath. "I think that's going to help me sleep better," he said.

"I thought it might."

"How did you know Woody infiltrated revolutionary groups here?" I asked the chief.

"That's where I was the other day," he said. "Took a little trip up to Texas to find out something of his background, although I have to say I couldn't connect the dots until you broke the code."

"Was it just the language thing that made you suspect Woody?" Olga asked.

"No," I said. "There were other details that were not critical by themselves but added to the big picture. For instance, Woody never put off his mail run for anyone. Guy Kovach said Woody refused to wait for him. 'The mail must go through,' he would say. Yet he waited through three postponements with Vaughan. Why? Because the whole trip was planned around Vaughan, taking him captive, and extorting a million dollars. If Woody was also a kidnap victim, you could hardy suspect him."

"So that irrational argument with the hotel clerk the morning we were to leave for home was just a way to make us late?" Vaughan asked.

"Exactly," I said. "He timed it so that you would come upon the simulated accident at a precise hour. He was used to planning military tactics, so he knew exactly how long to delay to get you to the kidnap site on time. That was important because otherwise he couldn't be assured that there wouldn't be others on the road, perhaps even a police patrol."

"But there *could* have been a police patrol," Olga said. "He couldn't have prevented that."

"True, but he knew their routine. He kept track of the police assignments by visiting the station house each time he went on a trip and checking out the duty assignments on the big board. They were used to seeing him report his upcoming trips. It never occurred to them that he might be there to gain information as well."

"You're making me cringe," Rivera said. "We were all pretty naïve."

"You couldn't have known," I said. "His visits were not something out of the ordinary. Plus, those motives are hard to spot."

"Let me ask you about the artist," the chief said. "We took her prints as you suggested and sent them to the lab that examined the letter. Threatened with exposure, she broke down and confessed. She told us a whole long story, but the bottom line was that she lost a lover in a political demonstration some fifteen years back and that converted her from a bystander to an active participant."

"Fifteen years ago, about the same time that you told me you first began to see signs of activity from the Revolutionary Guanajuato Brigade," I said.

He shook his head. "Right again."

"As you said, she didn't do much more than issue statements and threaten; she never took any action. I think she was more romantic than revolutionary. She painted her own face as an insurgent in many of the works she'd completed over the years. Recently, she'd begun to regret that. I think that's why she wanted to buy back the paintings in your living room, Vaughan. I'll bet if we look carefully, we'll find her face among the peasants holding the pitchforks and knives."

"I'm grateful she confessed," Olga said, "because I have to tell you, Jessica, that I was afraid your accusation wouldn't hold up. Lots of artists work in pen and ink, especially in this town. How could you be certain that her ink, and not some other artist's ink, was used to write the letter?"

"It was a guess, I'll admit, but an educated one. When you were away, the instant message from the kidnapper demanding ransom came from someone who styled himself 'Pelican.' I wracked my brain trying to figure out the significance of a seabird to the revolutionary cause."

"And so did I," Rivera said. "My wife and I spent an evening on the Internet trying to track down that one."

"And did you figure it out?" Vaughan asked.

I laughed. "Not exactly. But when I was at Sarah's and looked at the table with the array of pens and ink for her new projects, it became clear. The special materials for her pen-and-ink drawings were from a company called Pelikan. I thought that kind of irony would appeal to her."

"Caught in her own trap, in a way, like Woody," Vaughan said. "The one I feel sorry for is Philip. I had a feeling he had a crush on Sarah, but he turned his back on her last night. What do you think will happen to him now?"

"Dina told me that Woody had a life insurance policy," Olga said. "It's not large, but it's enough to let Philip go back to school, for at least a year or two. After that, he'll have to earn his way. By the way, they're leaving San Miguel for a while."

"The Fishers?" Vaughan asked. "I thought Roberto loved it here. Everyone thinks he's a native, or so he says."

"He loves it, but it hasn't been as easy for Dina. She's going into a rehab program."

"I'm sorry about that, but I have to say if I were married to Roberto, I'd probably need rehab, too."

"Vaughan. Be nice."

"What about Sarah?" I asked Chief Rivera. "Will she go to jail?"

"Don't know," he replied. "The American consulate is already making noise about sending her back to the States. Apparently her father is a wealthy man with connections." Rivera got to his feet and thrust out his hand to Vaughan. "Good to have you back in one piece. I hope the rest of your time in San Miguel is more peaceful."

"Thanks, Chief. You've got a rain check for dinner. I hope you'll cash it in and bring your wife and son."

"I'll check with them and let you know." He turned to me. "Señora Fletcher, the next time you're in San Miguel, I expect a visit. Captain Gutierrez hasn't stopped talking about you for two days. He says he's going to name his cat after you, because he's sure any cat named Jessica Fletcher will never let a mouse get away."

"And here I thought he didn't like me," I said.

We all laughed, and as if they heard us, the church bells of San Miguel de Allende began to chime, the sound now friendly and warm. I looked at the ring on my finger and thought of my *bandido*. Somewhere in the city was a father with a bad cough and two small children to care for, and I silently wished him well.

ABOUT THE AUTHORS

Jessica Fletcher is a bestselling mystery writer who has a knack for stumbling upon real-life mysteries in her various travels. **Donald Bain**, her longtime collaborator, is also the writer of more than eighty other books, many of them bestsellers. He can be contacted at www.donaldbain.com.